TEA IS FOR TRAITOR

KAREN SUE WALKER

LARAGRAY PRESS

ACKNOWLEDGMENTS

My gorgeous cover was designed by Mariah Sinclair, the Cozy Cover Queen. You can find her at https://www.thecovervault.com or on Facebook.

Thank you to Alyssa Lynn Palmer for your copyediting expertise. Also, many thanks to Stephen Santacroce for copyediting my recipes and answering my many culinary questions.

Special thanks to my beta readers, typo catchers, and early reviewers—I'm so grateful to you for your support!

Finally, to my wonderful readers. Keep on sending me those emails with suggestions, ideas, and pictures of your cats and dogs!

Sign up for email updates at https://karensuewalker.com and I'll do my best to keep your inbox full of everything cozy.

CHAPTER 1

Serenity Cove, the tiny seaside town I now called home, lived up to its name only during the summer months. Now, in October, powerful waves crashed against the rocks, throwing spray ten feet into the air. If a storm headed our way, the sea would become even more volatile.

"April May." Irma's scolding voice reminded me of my mother. "Are you just going to stand there? We're supposed to be getting exercise." She tapped her walking stick on a boulder for emphasis.

I glanced once more at the ocean, wild and untamed, and breathed deeply, filling my lungs with the salty sea air. Seagulls squawked as they soared overhead, scanning the beach for their breakfast.

"Fine," I said, and gestured for her to lead the way. I'd thought inviting my seventy-something friend to go for a morning walk meant that it would be a relaxing stroll, but Irma took fitness seriously since her recent health scare. There would be time to sit on the beach and watch the waves later.

We walked along the beach nearly to the lighthouse. Gazing up at the structure, I felt a pang in my chest remembering the woman who'd jumped from the platform and fallen to her death. I closed my eyes and said a silent prayer for her.

"No dwelling on sad memories." Irma grabbed me by the elbow and jerked her head in the direction of home. "Let's pick up the pace on the way back."

I put my hands on my hips. "Are you training for a marathon or something?"

She ignored my question. "Next time, we'll walk south to the hotel and back. I hope you appreciate me taking it easy on you."

"Easy?" I smirked. By the time I made it home, we would have walked two miles. I could handle that easily, but walking at a brisk pace on soft sand added a level of difficulty. My calves were already screaming at me.

We walked back to the pink and purple Victorian home that I'd turned into a tearoom. The rose bushes that surrounded the wide, wraparound porch sported their last blooms of the season.

I lived on the second floor and shared the house with Whisk, a Bengal cat, who lived in the attic, and the ghost of Chef Emile Toussaint, who seemed destined to spend eternity in my kitchen. My young assistant, Jennifer, rented a room from me. If I'd had children, I would have wanted a daughter just like her. As a bonus, she was a whiz with the espresso machine.

After parting ways with Irma at my front door, I hurried upstairs, took a quick shower, and dressed in a peach-toned flowered dress Jennifer had helped me pick out. She seemed to think as a tearoom proprietress, I should look the part. I slipped into coordinating ballet flats.

In the kitchen, I found Jennifer prepping food for the day. I pulled a few single-serving sized shepherd's pies out of the refrigerator and turned on the oven. A number of locals often stopped by for one of our lunch specials, helping to keep us profitable during the slow autumn. I hoped they'd do the same during the winter, when I'd been told to expect even fewer tourists.

Since the beginning of October, I'd cut back our hours. Now we opened only four days a week—Thursday through Sunday—giving Jennifer and me time to pursue some hobbies. The decision on which hobbies to pursue took up plenty of my time.

A glossy catalog sat on the kitchen counter. "What's this?" I asked.

Jennifer looked up from slicing cucumbers. "It's from Somerton community college. I was checking out their classes since I'm working fewer hours. I'm thinking of going back part time and maybe eventually I'll get a college degree."

"That's wonderful." I'd always known Jennifer was destined for greater things than helping me at my tearoom. "It's good to think about the future. What degree are you considering pursuing?"

She smiled shyly. "I'm not sure. Literature, history, art... I don't have to decide right now."

"No, you don't. Take all the classes you enjoy while you can. No reason to get stuck in a rut at your age."

"They have non-credit classes, too," she said. "You should check it out."

I picked up the catalog and leafed through it, pausing at the section with art classes. "I've always wanted to learn to paint."

She looked over my shoulder and read the description. "The class starts next Tuesday. You should sign up right now." The urgency of her voice surprised me.

"Have I been that annoying?" I asked.

Jennifer gave me a reassuring smile. "No, it's not that, but if you don't find another hobby besides cooking, we're going to run out of room in the walk-in freezer. And that's saying something. If we have a power outage, you'll have to invite everyone in town over to eat it all before it goes bad."

I nearly dropped my potholder. "I hope that never happens. Although it might be a good way to get to know more of my neighbors." I put four of the shepherd's pies in the oven and set the timer for thirty minutes. By then, the mashed potatoes should be nicely browned with the filling bubbling up around the edges. "But don't expect me to invite Ms. Grumpy Pants from next door."

Jennifer shrugged. "Mrs. Fadley isn't that bad." She must have seen my doubtful expression, because she added, "My mom always used to say that you never know what's going on in someone's life to make them act the way they do."

I scowled. "Fine. I'll give her the benefit of the doubt. For now."

"What happened with the photography?" Jennifer asked. "Didn't you buy yourself a new fancy camera?"

"Yes." An expensive one, along with several lenses, a tripod, and all the other items that the rather persuasive salesman at the camera shop insisted I'd need. A thought came to mind. "I can take pictures of the ocean and then paint them."

"Great idea," Jennifer agreed. "All you have to do is learn how to operate the camera."

I sighed. "I never knew hobbies were so much work."

My resident ghost, Chef Emile, shimmered into view. "You have yet to perfect a number of the techniques of French cooking," he said in a scolding tone. "This is not the time to allow yourself to become distracted."

"I can't spend all my time cooking," I said.

"I never said you could," Jennifer said with a puzzled look.

I chuckled. "Just me thinking out loud again."

Jennifer raised her eyebrows. "You do that a lot."

"I have been enjoying finding new recipes for the vegetables and herbs that someone keeps leaving on our doorstep. I'm curious if our anonymous vegetable fairy is going to leave anything over the winter months —maybe rutabagas or greens? I guess I'll just have to see."

Returning my attention to the brochure, I made up my mind to take the class. While learning to paint sounded like fun, my ulterior motive was to make some new friends. Lately, I'd spent most of my free time with a ghost and a cat. I enjoyed Jennifer's company, but since she'd reconnected with her long-lost grandmother, I didn't see her much outside of work hours these days. If she started taking college classes, I might not see her at all outside of work hours.

CHAPTER 2

From the moment we opened at noon, we were busy serving lunch to a lively crowd. As business began to slow, we got another rush for afternoon tea. Before I knew it, we were locking the front door and carrying the last of the dishes into the kitchen. Once the dishwasher had been filled and Jennifer swept the tearoom floor, she left to have Sunday dinner with her grandmother and father. I sat at the kitchen island eating the last shepherd's pie.

Chef Emile appeared in the corner, leaning against the counter and sipping a glass of wine.

"That looks good." I retrieved a bottle of Chardonnay from the refrigerator and poured myself a glass while Chef watched me carefully.

"You are having red meat for your dinner and white wine?" His tone expressed disapproval.

"Things are different these days," I said. "People drink what they want. I suppose an ale would have been a good choice, but I don't have any on hand. Besides, red wine gives me headaches."

Chef sniffed disapprovingly and pursed his lips.

I decided to change the subject. "Did you ever have any hobbies besides cooking?"

"I had no time for hobbies," he said. "And in my youth, there was little money for such frivolities."

"You didn't play an instrument?" I asked.

"Well, of course," he said. "There was not much else to do in the evenings when I was young. I was given an old guitar, and I plucked the strings, but I never did master it. It was not my passion."

"Cooking was your passion?"

"*Mais oui.*" He smiled broadly. "Cooking and women."

I blinked, not knowing how to respond. Chef had always seemed like a one-woman man. In his youth, he'd fallen in love with a French woman who'd passed away. Later, when he'd come to Serenity Cove in the nineteen-sixties, he'd been desperately in love with the previous owner, Norma. I suspected she'd led him on for years to keep him working for her when my home had housed a popular French restaurant. "Were there many women?"

"Yes, of course. It is very difficult to remember all of them."

"Oh." I sat in silence for a moment, and then Chef smiled slyly and winked. Did that mean he'd been pulling my leg?

I watched him as he put down the wineglass and pulled out the little notebook he'd been writing in lately. Whether he worked on his memoirs or another cookbook, he refused to tell me about his project in spite of my many questions.

I carried my dishes to the sink. "I'm going to bring Whisk his dinner," I said, but he didn't look up. "Maybe you can tell me about all your women later."

I took a scoop of cat food and a bottle of filtered water up the back stairs, down the hall, and up to the attic.

"Whisk?" I called out. I refilled his bowls and took a seat in his favorite Windsor chair. It was covered in cat hair, and I scolded myself for forgetting a lint brush. Again.

When I'd first moved in, I'd fixed the broken panes on the attic windows and tried to lure Whisk to the lower floors. He'd wailed and moaned until I finally opened one of the attic windows a crack so he could continue to come and go as he pleased. He rarely came downstairs, but I hoped someday he'd feel safe and comfortable enough to spend time in the rest of the house.

The Bengal cat appeared from behind a box, his sleek, spotted coat glistening in the dim light of the single fixture. After regarding me for a moment with narrowed eyes, he strolled over to his dish and sniffed the food. He literally turned up his nose and focused his gaze on me.

"I'm sorry, but that's what the vet said I should feed you," I explained. "Besides, you don't appear to be wasting away."

Whisk flopped on the floor and began licking his front paw.

"I'm thinking of taking up painting as a hobby," I said. "I can only do so much cooking and baking. Now that we're only open four days a week instead of six, I have a lot more time on my hands. Do you have any hobbies, Whisk?" The cat was a surprisingly good listener, though his responses to my inquiries were limited.

Whisk approached me but slipped past the chair and maneuvered between the boxes and old furniture. About the time I'd decided he didn't want to talk about his extracurricular activities, he reappeared with a small critter in his mouth.

Startled, I jumped to my feet and squealed. I must have startled Whisk too, since his mouth dropped open, and the creature scampered away. Whisk ran after it, but returned in a few minutes empty handed, or perhaps empty pawed would be more accurate.

Once my breathing calmed, I said, "Oh, right. I suppose hunting is an appropriate hobby for an independent cat like you. Do you have any other fun things you like to do that aren't quite so... gruesome?"

Whisk tilted his head to one side as if he didn't understand the question, then rubbed up against my legs.

"Are you lonely up here all by yourself?" I asked. "I get lonely sometimes. I mean at first, I was so busy with the tearoom and, well, other things." Like murders. There'd been an unusual number of dead bodies in town since I moved here, but I'd been assured that wasn't a normal situation.

"Jennifer isn't around as much since her grand-mother moved to town," I continued, "and now she's planning to start taking college classes. I can always stop in and see Irma at the Mermaid Cafe, of course, but she's working and doesn't always have time to talk. And I'm starting to wonder if Freddie is getting serious about someone. She's such a private person, if she is in a relationship, I'll probably find out when I get my wedding invitation."

Whisk mewed in response, then wandered off to another part of the attic.

"No, you're too independent to be lonely," I contin-ued. "It must be nice to be a cat, as long as you have someone bringing you food regularly. You don't have to make a living or do much of anything you don't want to."

I laughed at myself for expecting a cat to keep me company. Clearly, Whisk had other things on his mind than chatting with me. What I needed was some new friends.

TUESDAY ARRIVED before I knew it, and I found myself at Somerton Community College lost in a maze of hallways.

A woman's voice from behind me asked, "Are you looking for the watercolor class?"

I swung around to see a stylish woman around my

age coming toward me. As she came closer, I decided she couldn't possibly be fifty like me unless she'd had some work done. She had an air of confidence from her posture to her lip-glossed smile. Her layered honey-blonde hair fell to her shoulders, not a strand out of place. The crisp white shirt she wore looked even whiter against her tan skin.

"Yes," I smiled, hoping she didn't notice the stain on my shirt. I'd worn old clothes, assuming others would do the same. "Are you learning to paint too?"

"Perhaps someday I'll master the skill, but I come to class for the social interaction." She pointed the way, and I walked alongside her. "I'm Cheryl. I'll introduce you to the girls."

We stepped inside the room and Cheryl turned to me. "How silly. I forgot to ask your name."

"I'm April," I said. "April May."

Her smile evaporated as her eyebrows rose nearly an inch. "*You're* April May?" Her eyes swiftly scanned me from top to toe, and then her smile returned. "You're not at all what I'd expected."

My face scrunched up in discomfort, wondering why she'd recognized my name. Had I fallen short of someone's description?

Doing my best to sound casual, I asked, "Do we have a mutual friend?"

"I didn't tell you my last name, did I?" she said. "I'm Cheryl Fontana. Sheriff Fontana's wife."

CHAPTER 3

hile I tried to hide my surprise, Cheryl introduced me to the other "girls," who greeted me with warm smiles, calming my nerves a bit.

Debbie stood no more than five feet tall, and I wondered how she'd found designer clothing to fit her tiny frame, but then she could probably afford a tailor to alter her entire wardrobe. Her pixie cut suited the brunette perfectly.

"Debbie's husband is state representative Joe Jorgensen," Cheryl explained.

"Here, you can set up next to me." Debbie motioned to the easel next to her. "I've got plenty of brushes and paints you can borrow, and I'll help you make a list of what to buy. You don't need a lot to get started, but I got a little carried away, as you can see."

"Thanks," I said gratefully, eyeing her elegant oak case overflowing with tubes of paint.

"And this is Sandra Vitello." Cheryl pronounced her name Sahn-drah. The blonde wore false eyelashes and a fuchsia shade of lipstick on puffed-up lips. Cheryl put a protective arm around Sandra's shoulders and explained that she'd recently married Eric Vitello, the vice president of a local tech company. "She's the newest member of the club," she added.

"Oh, you're in a club." I simultaneously wanted nothing to do with a club of wealthy wives and yet hoped I'd be asked to join.

Cheryl laughed. "It's just an expression. Although our book club meets at the Somerton library once a month. You'll have to come by and meet the rest of the girls."

I grinned awkwardly. "Sure. Sounds great."

Had I unknowingly stepped into an episode of *The Real Housewives*? If the women started screaming at each other and pulling hair, that would be my clue to get out quickly.

Or maybe this was more like the movie *Mean Girls*. Would these women cause me to lose track of my moral compass and sacrifice my friends to be part of the popular group? I nearly laughed out loud at the thought. *You've got quite an imagination, April.*

The teacher called out for our attention and introduced himself as Ron Alexander. He looked more like an accountant than an artist, with his close-cropped hair and wire-framed glasses. He'd rolled up the sleeves of his plaid, cotton shirt.

Besides Cheryl, Debbie, and Sandra, I spotted several more women and a few men. Many of them seemed to know each other at least casually.

"I see some new faces," Ron said. "Welcome. This

class is for all levels, so don't worry if you've never painted before. We'll have you creating art in no time at all."

While he explained our first project—a simple tree —Cheryl and her friends pulled on matching aprons over their heads to protect their clothing. I'd have to bring one next time—that would mean I could wear nicer clothes. Cheryl and Debbie began squeezing tubes of paint onto plastic trays and dipping their brushes into water, while Sandra watched them, following their lead and ignoring the instructor.

"The leaves of your tree can be any color you wish," Ron instructed. "For first timers, I recommend starting with just three colors. For the tree trunk, you'll want raw umber or burnt umber, or a combination of the two for my returning students. You can use any blue you like for the sky such as cerulean blue or cobalt blue if you prefer a deeper, more vibrant sky. And for the leaves, a viridian green would be lovely, or use your imagination. Perhaps your tree is covered in pink or purple blossoms."

My new friends agreed they wanted pink trees, so I went along with their decision, squeezing paint onto my borrowed palette.

CHAPTER 4

On our morning beach walk, I told Irma about meeting the sheriff's wife, Cheryl, along with Debby and Sandra as we passed by the pier and Irma's restaurant, the Mermaid Cafe.

"Just don't forget who your real friends are," Irma said.

"What does that mean?" I asked. "Are you afraid you'll be replaced as my partner in crime solving?"

She came to a sudden stop and gave me a quizzical look. "Are you expecting more crime? Haven't we had enough around here?"

"We've had quite enough." Especially the murders. "But don't worry. You were the first friend I made when I came to town, and we'll always be friends."

"Who said I was worried?" Irma took off at her usual brisk pace and I hurried to keep up. We reached the beach in front of the hotel, and I plopped down on the sand in front of a row of chaise lounges they'd set up for guests. It seemed unlikely that they'd have many of their guests sunbathing on this chilly October day, but you never knew about Midwesterners. I'd heard they had thicker blood.

"Are you just going to sit here?" Irma asked.

"My calves are killing me," I said. "I just need a moment. Or an hour. Come to think of it, I might ask the hotel staff to call me a cab." I rubbed my arms to warm them. "It's cold out here."

Irma perched on the end of one of the chaise lounges. "You are such a lightweight," she grumbled. "I need to get some younger friends."

A woman wearing a white shirt and black slacks appeared out of nowhere. "May I get you something? A mimosa perhaps?"

Before I could say no, Irma responded enthusiastically. "A mimosa sounds great. Bring her one too. She's paying," she added.

I barely managed not to roll my eyes before nodding to the server. "Anything to keep her quiet."

The server chuckled as she went to get our drinks.

"I kind of thought the sheriff had an interest in you," Irma said, once we had our mimosas. "And you went all giggly when you were around him. Do you think he's happily married?"

I scoffed. "Happy or not, he's off limits."

"That doesn't stop plenty of people." When I didn't respond to her bait, she added, "I'm glad to know it stopped you. And him. Even though I didn't vote for him. The assistant sheriff is a lot cuter." She lifted a finger as if a thought had just occurred to her. "Hey, I think he's single. You should go out with him."

"Thanks for the suggestion, Emma."

"Huh?" Irma cocked her head. "The name's Irma. Did you hit your head or something?"

"Emma, from the book by Jane Austen," I clarified. "She was an interfering matchmaker. Jennifer's got me reading all of her books."

The server reappeared. "Would you like to order breakfast? Our eggs Benedict is to die for."

"Yes," Irma said.

"No," I said to the server, adding to Irma, "If you're going to order anything, it should be poached eggs and dry toast."

Irma sulked and waved off the server. "Never mind."

"You told me to help you with your dietary restrictions," I said. After Irma's health scare when she thought she'd had a heart attack, her doctor had told her she'd need to change her eating habits and exercise more.

She frowned and shook her head. "What's the point of living if you can't have any fun?"

"Maybe *you* should go on a date with the assistant sheriff," I suggested, moving my chair farther away so she couldn't kick me.

To my surprise, her face lit up. "That's a great idea. I mean, not the assistant sheriff, but maybe you could help me get on one of those dating websites, or the app where you swipe right if you think a guy's hot."

"Really?" I asked. Irma had never talked about dating or being interested in anyone, but maybe that was because she knew everyone in town.

"Really. There aren't any eligible men in town I'd want to date. Unless… Do you think your handyman is too young for me?"

"Irma!"

"Calm down," she said. "I thought you too had decided not to give it a go. Has that changed?"

I didn't like talking about my personal life, but that wouldn't stop Irma from nagging me until she got an answer. "Mark and I have decided to be friends."

She waved her hand as if to say, "go on."

"He was kind of freaked out about the ghost thing," I admitted. "I didn't plan to tell him, but I'm glad he found out now." Irma was one of the few people who knew I could see ghosts.

She patted me on the leg. "Sorry to hear that. He sure was hot, but he's not the only fish in the sea. Maybe we could double date."

I laughed. "Let's find you a man first. Maybe he'll have a son or nephew I can go out with."

"That's the spirit."

Making Irma a dating profile wasn't the craziest idea I'd ever heard, and if it kept her mind off unhealthy food, it might be a welcome distraction.

"You'll have to get a new phone, you know," I said. "You can't swipe right on a flip phone."

Irma downed the last of her drink and stood. "Let's head home. No time like the present."

～

AFTER IRMA and I drove to Somerton to get her new phone, we came back to my place to set it up. I did my best to make everything user friendly, which wasn't easy once she found the app store and started downloading games.

Jennifer found us in the kitchen drinking tea. "What are you two up to?"

"I'm up to level nine in Candy Crush," Irma said.

I sighed. "I'm signing Irma up for a dating app. Or at least I'm trying. She has the attention span of a gnat."

"Which app?" Jennifer asked.

Irma stared at her screen. "April suggested OK Stupid, but I nixed that idea. I prefer smart men. eCodgers sounded promising, but all the men were looking for someone to take care of them in their old age."

"You're making that up," Jennifer said, hesitantly adding, "Aren't you?"

"Maybe." Irma said, noncommittally. "We settled on SelectSeniors." She showed Jennifer the screen. "That guy looks like he can still get his motor running, doesn't he?"

Jennifer's eyes widened and her cheeks reddened. "I just remembered I have to... do something." She hurried from the room.

"Was it something I said?" Irma asked.

I was too busy laughing to answer. When I was able to speak, I said, "I think you embarrassed her."

"Why?" Irma shook her head slowly. "Young people. They think they're the only ones interested in getting some." She showed me the screen. "Would you Netflix and chill with him?"

"Is that a euphemism?" I asked.

She grinned. "It might be. But I never kiss and tell." She stood and set her teacup next to the sink.

"Tomorrow, same time, same place?" I asked.

"I'm busy tomorrow," She headed for the back door.

"Busy doing what?" I asked. Irma never kept secrets from me before. "Oh, do you have a date?"

"Dance class," she said. "I'd invite you, but we're in the middle of rehearsals for our debut at the Winter Holiday Festival."

"You're in a dance troupe?" If anyone would still be dancing in their seventies, it would be Irma. "Why didn't I know this?"

"Do you have to know everything?" Irma stepped out the back door, and I followed her down the sidewalk toward the driveway.

I didn't *have* to know everything, but I certainly preferred to. "Are you sure I can't come?" Dancing sounded like fun, and besides, I wanted to find a new hobby and get more exercise. Dance class would accomplish both goals. "What kind of dancing is it? Ballet? Jazz?"

Irma stopped and turned to face me. "We're calling ourselves the Sextettes. Like the Rockettes, only sexier."

"Well, obviously," I said with a laugh. "I suppose I'm not sexy enough for your group." I smiled innocently.

"Can you do a high kick?" she asked. When I hesitated, she ordered me to show her.

I took one step forward and swung my leg up, but my foot didn't even make it as high as my waist.

"We need to work on that," Irma said. "I'll pick you up tomorrow morning at eight."

CHAPTER 5

The next morning, I dressed in a T-shirt and leggings as Irma had instructed me. She texted from the driveway, and when I didn't immediately appear, she honked. Jennifer had made Irma a mocha and me a cappuccino, and I carried the two travel mugs out to her car.

Once buckled in, I asked where the classes were held.

"At the community center," she said.

"We have a community center?" I thought I knew about every business and building in our little town.

"Sort of. It's a room at city hall across from the mayor's office. We're working on getting our own building, but Mayor Gasden fights us every step of the way."

Mayor Gasden had been a thorn in my side since I first met her, and I was sure she felt the same way about me. I'd kept her from turning our library into a food court, and she still scowled every time she saw me.

The mayor's office shared a building with the police station and all other city functions. Irma parked, and we made our way through the door and down a long hall to room 203. I followed Irma into the room.

The six women stopped talking and stared at us.

"No interlopers!" one older woman called out, and everyone started talking at once.

I turned and met the glaring woman's gaze. "Mrs. Fadley?" Mrs. Fadley, aka Mrs. Grumpy Pants, was the last person I'd expected to see at a dance class. She stuck her tongue out at me.

A petite, dark-haired, forty-ish woman clapped her hands, attempting to get everyone's attention. By her demeanor, I guessed her to be the instructor. "Order, ladies!" she bellowed, surprisingly loud for someone so small.

When the chatter continued, she clapped again and yelled even louder, "I said order!" Everyone stopped talking immediately, and she continued in a normal voice. "I'm disappointed in all of you. When we have a visitor, I expect you to welcome them, just as you were once welcomed."

A few women grumbled "hello" and "welcome" in my direction. The instructor lined us up in two rows, pulling me into the front. She ran us through a few moves, and I was shocked to see how high some of the seniors could kick. Irma could have kicked someone in their chin if she wanted to. In a pinch, I might have been able to kick someone in the crotch. I hoped I didn't need that move anytime soon.

Irma must have seen my frustration, because she jabbed me with her bony elbow. "It just takes practice. And stretching."

"Got it," I said. "I can practice."

"And stretch," Irma repeated, sliding into the splits.

"Show off," I mumbled, but I knew Irma heard me by the sparkle in her eyes.

AFTER CLASS, I invited Irma over for breakfast and Jennifer offered us another round of espresso drinks. Jennifer set my cappuccino on the island and then went about making Irma her non-fat, decaf latte.

Irma nibbled on the yolk-free egg bites I'd made with turkey bacon. She appeared less than enthusiastic.

I took a bite of one. "These aren't half bad."

"They're edible," Irma said with a scowl. Then she gave me one of her goofy smiles. "Sorry, but I miss bacon. And all the other yummy food that I can't have anymore. I do appreciate you making these."

"My pants have been getting snug around the waist, so I'm happy to try out some lo-cal recipes."

"Can I try one too?" Jennifer asked.

Irma shook her head. "If you turned sideways, you'd disappear."

I smacked Irma's arm with a dishtowel. "You're never too young to start eating healthy." I handed Jennifer one of the bites.

Irma pulled out her new smart phone. "You two can help me pick out candidates to be my new beau."

"Sure," Jennifer said as she began her daily task of slicing cucumbers. I assembled a few prosciutto, apple, and brie tea sandwiches. I handed one each to Jennifer and Irma to taste.

"What do you think?" I asked.

"Ooh, I like the crispness of the apple," Jennifer said.

Irma stared at the little sandwich on the plate in front of her. "If I'm allowed to eat this, it must not be any good."

"One won't hurt you," I said.

"One?" she groused. "But it's so tiny."

"You're right." I reached for the plate. "I shouldn't tease you with one tiny sandwich when you can't have seconds."

Irma snatched up the sandwich and stuffed the whole thing in her mouth. Looking like a squirrel with its cheeks full of nuts, she grinned and held up two thumbs.

In the early afternoon, we had a few locals in for lunch. Almost everyone complained about my decision to stay closed three days a week. There weren't many places to eat lunch in our little town, but they'd survive as they had before I'd opened my tearoom.

A few guests dropped in over the next few hours for afternoon tea. While I cleaned up in the kitchen, Jennifer finished serving our last guests.

She stuck her head in the kitchen door. "Some women are asking for you."

"Who are they?" I asked.

Jennifer shrugged. "Never saw them before in my life."

I wiped my hands on a dishtowel, took off my apron, and went to greet them. Just inside the front door, Cheryl, Debbie, and Sandra stood with another woman I hadn't met. All four were impeccably dressed down to their designer shoes.

Cheryl glided forward to greet me wearing an elegant pantsuit. "I hope you don't mind us dropping in like this. I just had to see your tearoom." She rotated in place to take in the decor, then announced, "It's darling."

"You're right," Debbie chimed in. "That's the perfect word for it. Darling."

I smiled, hoping they meant it as a compliment. "Thank you. Would you like a table?"

"We really can't stay for more than a few minutes," Cheryl said, acting as the group's spokesperson. "I wouldn't want you to go to any trouble."

"Have a seat by the window," I said, "and I'll bring you some tea and sandwiches."

"Only if you're sure it's no trouble," Debbie added.

"This is a tearoom," I said with a grin, hoping it didn't sound sarcastic. "It's no trouble at all."

"You are a dear," Cheryl said, then turned to her friends. "Isn't she a dear?"

They nodded and agreed that I was "a dear."

"Any dietary restrictions or allergies?" I asked.

To my surprise, not one of the women was vegan, gluten intolerant, or on a raw diet.

"Please don't bring too much," Debbie requested. "It's so close to dinner. And nothing too fattening."

"Yes," Cheryl agreed. "Just a few nibbles would be lovely."

Sandra wore a smile that didn't waver, and she spoke no more than a few words, much like she'd done at the painting class. She'd changed her hairstyle, parting it on the side and draping it over one eye the way the actress Veronica Lake had once done. Her makeup was toned down from when I'd met her at painting class, and I wondered if that was Cheryl's influence.

The other woman appeared much younger—maybe in her late twenties, though looks could be deceiving. "I don't believe we've met. I'm April May." Her dark hair fell in waves past her tiny waist, and I would have bet they were extensions.

"That's Bree," Cheryl informed me with a wave of her hand.

"Nice to meet you," Bree said shyly, petting her long hair like an emotional support animal.

I led them to the round table by the window and hurried back to the kitchen. Putting on the kettle, I asked Jennifer to help me arrange some platters of sandwiches for the women to share.

"And desserts?" she asked.

After thinking for a moment, I said, "Yes, I bet they'll gobble them up." My experience told me that the women who protested they didn't want dessert were the ones who'd been depriving themselves of the pleasure, sometimes for years.

I readied two teapots, one with my favorite rose petal black tea and one with a fall herbal blend I'd created myself with chamomile, cinnamon, cardamon, and other spices. Jennifer took the ladies teacups and place settings, and I soon followed carrying a tray with their teapots.

I set the first pot on the table. "The rose petal tea has a base of *Keemun*, a popular Chinese black tea. It is caffeinated, so you might want to go easy on it if you want to get to sleep tonight. This pot," I said as I set a brown and orange teapot next to the first, "is a fall, herbal mixture with chamomile as its base, and it has no caffeine."

"How thoughtful," Cheryl said, beaming as if I'd done something extra special.

Jennifer arrived with two platters, one with a tea sandwich assortment and one filled with cookies and tarts. She handed them to me and then disappeared back into the kitchen.

"This is a sampling of our afternoon tea sandwich and dessert selections. Normally, I would also include mini-quiches, cream puffs, and Victorian sponge cake, but I didn't want you to spoil your dinners. Enjoy!"

As I turned to go, Debbie spoke up. "Won't you join us?"

My eyes went to Cheryl, who I thought of as the ringleader.

"Oh, yes," Cheryl said with a warm smile. "Bring over another teacup and pull up a chair. Your feet must be killing you after standing all day in those shoes."

I glanced at my feet. "Oh, these are quite comfortable, actually." I almost told her the discount store where I'd bought them until I noticed the red sole of one of Cheryl's pumps. "But, sure. I'd love to join you. I'll be right back."

Returning to the kitchen, Jennifer looked up from loading the dishwasher as I grabbed my favorite teacup.

"They asked me to join them," I said.

"In their cult?" she asked.

"What?"

She snickered. "I thought you had to be married to be in the rich wives' club. Did you see the purses?" She must have seen the disappointed look on my face, because she added, "I'm sure they're very nice. You can be rich and nice, too, right?" She gave me one of her sweetest smiles.

"Of course," I answered, and returned to the table. I pulled up a chair between Debbie and Sandra and poured myself a cup of tea.

The women gobbled up the sandwiches and treats like they hadn't eaten all day.

"This cucumber sandwich is just like they serve it at the Ritz," Debbie said.

"Which one?" Cheryl asked. "In Dubai, they serve a lovely traditional afternoon tea. Or at least they did when I was last there, but that was so long ago." She directed her next comment at me. "My father founded Maynard Industries. He traveled a great deal for business and often took me along until I got married." She sighed. "I was in such a hurry to settle down and have my own home. I wish I'd waited. Have you ever married?"

I nearly spit out my tea. "No. I never met the right man." I decided not to go into my failed engagement since the breakup still stung. "Maybe if I hadn't been so focused on my career…"

"That's exactly what I was telling Sandra," Cheryl said. "You really can't have a successful relationship and a successful career."

"Oh, I didn't mean—" I began.

"Yes, I know there are exceptions," Cheryl continued. "But when you marry the vice president of Maynard Industries, something has to give."

Sandra stared at her hands, almost cowering in her chair next to me.

I gently nudged her. "You haven't tried one of my freshly baked scones with house-made clotted cream. I've been told it's just as good as anything you'd find in England." Or Dubai, I thought. I whispered, "We'll talk later."

She glanced at me, smiled, and reached for a scone. I handed her the crock with the clotted cream which she slathered onto her scone.

When the women had devoured nearly everything on the platters, Debbie asked about my family.

"My mother passed away last year," I said. "That's when I moved to Serenity Cove. I wanted a fresh start. My only living relative is my brother, but I'm afraid we're not on good terms."

The women nodded knowingly, as if they knew all about dysfunctional family relationships.

"I enjoyed the painting class. Do you have any other

hobbies you think I might be interested in? I made the decision to reduce the hours of the tearoom during the off season, and now that we're only open four days a week, I feel like I have so much time on my hands."

"I love whales," Bree said, speaking up for the first time since I'd joined them at the table. "And dolphins. Do you have binoculars? I bet you can see them from your front porch. I'd get nothing at all done if I lived here."

"How about volunteering?" Cheryl asked. "We could use you at the Community Action Partnership. Or you could help out at the food bank on Saturday mornings."

"That's a great idea," I said, wondering what I was getting myself in for. "But not Saturdays. The week-ends are our busiest days."

"Oh, of course," Debbie said. "But watch out for Cheryl. She can be very persuasive."

After the women left, I went to the upstairs parlor which also served as my office to practice my kicks. I did hamstring stretches and tried a modified version of the splits. I had a long way to go before I could kick as high as Irma.

It seemed silly that I couldn't keep up with a seventy-something woman. I picked up a couple of Jennifer's books and held them like weights while I did some squats. Then more stretches and more kicks. I penciled a little mark on the wall so I could keep track of my high-kicking progress.

CHAPTER 6

*B*y the time Sunday rolled around, my legs hurt from all the stretching and kicking. I might have overdone it in a misguided attempt to compete with Irma. That, on top of being on my feet all day running the tearoom, and I was exhausted.

When a text arrived from Cheryl asking if I'd like to join her, Debbie, Sandra, and Bree for brunch, I had no problem saying no. Besides, I'd already told her that my busy weekends didn't leave time for other activities.

"You could go," Jennifer said. "I can get everything ready. As long as you're back in time to clean up…" She winked. She knew that cleaning up was my least favorite part of the job.

"No, I think I need a break from the ladies of leisure. Do you know that Cheryl doesn't think a woman can have a happy marriage and a successful career? At least not if you're married to an important businessman, apparently."

"Is that so?" Jennifer pulled a stack of cloth napkins

from a basket and began wrapping them around silverware. "Does that mean if I find a husband I can drop out of college?"

"Nope. You'll need all your knowledge to entertain your husband in the evening after he comes home from a long day of work."

She stopped in the middle of napkin folding. "Do people really think that way?"

I chuckled. "They did when I was young. My mother told me some of her friends went to college to get their M.R.S."

"M.R.S.?" She looked confused, and then it dawned on her. "Oh, Mrs. So, they went to college to find a husband? With no plans of going to work?"

"But with nearly half of marriages ending in divorce, I bet a lot of them were glad to have a college degree when they needed to find a job. Of course, it's still tough to get hired when the only experience you have is running a household and raising children."

Jennifer sighed. "It's not easy being a woman, is it? You'd think that having so many choices would be a good thing. But I feel like we're all expected to be superheroes."

I nodded. "That may be true, but I enjoy being a woman."

"Me, too." She grinned. "We get afternoon tea, pretty dresses, and the best books. Besides, I'd rather watch Bridgerton or The Gilded Age than football."

I raised my eyebrows. "Those are TV shows, right?"

"You haven't watched either of them?" she asked.

"The costumes are to die for." Jennifer had a fondness for period costumes that bordered on obsession.

"I'll have to check them out then." I had a thought. "Have you ever sewn costumes?" When she gave a shake of the head in response, I said, "I used to sew my own clothes when I was a kid. Maybe making period costumes would be a fun hobby."

Her eyes widened. "I've heard it's a lot of work, but if you want to try, I'll help. I never learned to sew."

"I'll add that to my list of potential hobbies." I pulled out a small spiral notebook from the junk drawer and flipped through the pages, finally finding it. "Ah, here it is." I added "making period costumes" to the list and handed the notebook to Jennifer.

She stared at it for a moment. "You have nearly everything on this list except skydiving."

I took the list back from her and added "skydiving" at the bottom.

Jennifer looked over my shoulder. "You're going to need to live a long time just to try everything on that list once."

"You're right," I said, and crossed off "skydiving."

My phone buzzed, and I picked it up to look at the text. *The dolphins are running. Should see from your porch.* I didn't recognize the number, but I guessed it must be from Bree after our conversation at tea.

"Want to check out the dolphins?" I asked.

Jennifer begged off. "You go ahead. Give me a yell if you see them."

I went upstairs and found my brand-new camera. I'd splurged on a zoom lens, so I figured this would be a good time to try it out. Grabbing a sweatshirt, I went out on the front porch and got comfortable in a spot with a good view of the ocean. The fog had burned off early, and a few fluffy white clouds floated by.

The camera was heavy, so instead of going back upstairs for the tripod, I rested the camera on the porch railing.

Some sort of a whirring sound caught my attention. It grew to a loud buzz, and I looked up at the sky as a small plane approached, one of those with the wings above the cockpit. I put my eyes to the camera viewfinder and took a picture so I could ask someone what kind of plane it was. I'd crossed skydiving off my list of potential hobbies, but maybe learning to fly a plane would be fun. Expensive too, no doubt.

I might give aerial photography a try. Or have someone take me up in their plane and so I could shoot pictures of Serenity Cove from above.

The plane droned on as it flew leisurely by. I gasped as something dropped from the plane. I had enough presence of mind to take a photo.

It was one thing to throw a cigarette butt out a car window, and I could rant for an hour about how bad that was for the environment with all the tobacco and nicotine and other chemicals being washed down storm drains into the ocean. But to throw trash from a plane directly into the ocean? That was a new low.

I glared at the plane as it flew into the distance, then stomped inside.

Jennifer was in the middle of arranging plates and

tea trays and looked up as I entered the kitchen. "What's wrong? No dolphins?"

"Worse." I set the camera down on the counter and pulled my apron over my head. "Someone just dumped something from a plane into the ocean. Can you imagine?"

She carried several tiered trays to the island. Her eyebrows drew together in a question. "Really? What was it? Could you tell?"

"No, but I got a picture." I examined the image in the camera's digital display. "It was probably five or six feet long and not very wide. Like a…" The idea came to me, but I didn't want to believe it.

Jennifer waited for me to finish my sentence, but when I didn't, she prompted me. "Like a… what?"

I sighed. "Like a body."

CHAPTER 7

While Jennifer finished with the day's preparations, I went up to my office to download the photo from my camera. Since this was the first time I'd done it, it took me nearly an hour. I printed out the picture of the plane, enlarged as much as I could without losing too much quality, and the picture of whatever had been dropped from it.

I took both photos downstairs to show Jennifer.

"I don't know," she said. "It's hard to tell what it is. I mean it *could* be a body, but it could be any number of other things, too."

"Don't get me wrong," I said. "I very much hope it's not a body. But I'm going to call the police and report it either way."

When I called our local police station, I learned that Deputy Molina had regained his position as the acting police chief for Serenity Cove. I left a message for him to call me.

The picture-perfect weather brought the crowds from neighboring towns to Serenity Cove. They lined the street from the hotel to the lighthouse with their cars. Many of them stopped in our tearoom for lunch or afternoon tea, and we had to turn some away. I was so busy making extra sandwiches and baking scones and cookies, I didn't see Molina had called back until the end of the day. As I hit redial, Jennifer came into the kitchen.

"Deputy Molina is here," she said, but before I could get up, he appeared behind her in the kitchen doorway. I'd almost forgotten how young he looked with his round baby face and dark, unruly hair. "I'll finish up out front." Jennifer disappeared into the tearoom and the door swung closed behind her.

"Deputy, come in and have a seat." I motioned to one of the stools. "Would you like a cup of tea? I just made a pot."

"Can you put that over ice?" he asked. "It's hot today."

I hid my amusement as I made him a glass of iced tea. The mid-seventies would be considered hot only by Serenity Cove residents, but I didn't correct him. In the short time I'd lived in town, I'd gotten used to the cooler oceanside temperatures, too.

"What's this about someone dropping something from a plane?" he asked as he took a big gulp of tea.

I showed him the two pictures and didn't share my thoughts that the object appeared to be the size of a body.

He stared at the photo of the plane. "I can't make

out the N-number on the plane. Is this the best picture you took?"

"N-number?"

"Yeah. Every plane has an identifying number on the side. In the U.S., they start with an 'n'."

I took a closer look at the picture, trying to make out the numbers or letters. "I guess that's an 'n', but I'm not sure if the next number is an eight or a three. Can't you digitally enhance it or something?"

He scowled and shook his head. "That's only on TV shows. You can't enhance anything more than what the original pixels show."

"Oh." Not being sure what a pixel was, I took his word for it.

"Maybe someone else got a better photo. Or maybe you can check with the local airports and see who took off this morning."

Molina shook his head. "Finding a litterbug is not high on the department's priority. I have to report to Sheriff Fontana, and he'd have me demoted if I spent more than an hour or two on this."

"Really?" I hesitated. "Even if it's not just some normal sort of trash they threw out of the plane?"

"What are you talking about?" His voice rose in frustration. "What do you think it was? Nuclear waste? Priceless antiquities? Or drugs?"

"No." With his attitude, I almost didn't tell him my suspicions. But he was our police chief, and he needed to know. "It might have been a body."

"A body?" he began to snicker and then the snicker

grew into a full-fledged laugh. "Ms. May, you have quite an imagination. I'll admit that lately dead bodies have turned up more often than is typically expected, but this —" he pointed to the picture of the item falling through the sky. For a moment he stared at it, not saying anything. He gave his head a little shake and continued. "That's just some junk that someone wanted to get rid of and was too lazy and cheap to haul to the dump."

"Too lazy to go to the dump so they took it to the airport and put it in a plane so they could drop it in the ocean?"

His eyebrows came together in a stern expression, but his shoulders slumped. That told me he thought I might be right.

"Email the files to me and I'll have a closer look," he said.

"Don't go telling everyone in town you saw a dead body in the sky."

As soon as we'd washed the last teacup of the day, I strolled on the sidewalk that led along the beach to the Mermaid Cafe. The pictures were safely tucked away in my purse. Molina had told me not to tell *everyone* about the plane, but he didn't say I couldn't tell a few close friends.

As many times as I'd been to Irma's cafe, stepping through the doors still felt like entering another world, with the undulating aqua and violet lights, giant clamshell chairs, and acrylic bar filled with sand, seaweed, and realistic-looking sea creatures.

I found my way to the bar and pulled up a stool. Irma soon appeared in her mermaid costume, complete with a long multi-colored wig.

"What'll it be?" she asked, and I ordered a glass of pinot grigio.

While she poured the wine, I pulled the pictures out, unfolded them, and flattened out the wrinkles.

She set the glass in front of me. "What have you got there?"

"While I was hoping to spot dolphins this morning, I saw something fall out of a plane. Luckily, I happened to be looking through the viewfinder and snapped a picture. I also got a picture of the plane." I pushed both pictures across the bar so she could get a good look.

"Hmmm," she murmured as she squinted at the first photo. She left and returned with reading glasses, then examined the other picture. "That's a Cessna 172."

"Really?" Now we were getting somewhere. "Do you know who owns it?"

She chuckled. "That plane's been in production for decades. There are probably thousands of them in operation." She went back to the first picture. "What's that supposed to be."

"That was pushed out of the plane." I leaned over the bar and whispered, "I think it's a body."

She snorted a laugh. "That?" She pointed at the object in the picture. "That could be anything."

"Like what?" I asked, sincerely wanting another theory that made more sense than mine.

Irma shrugged. "Um, I don't know. A rolled-up carpet?"

"With a body inside?"

Irma shook her head. "Look, Nancy Drew. You've been getting quite a reputation for finding bodies and that sort of thing lately, but that doesn't mean you should expect dead bodies to turn up every few weeks. This is Serenity Cove, not Cabot Cove."

"Cabot Cove?" I asked.

"Don't tell me you never watched *Murder She Wrote*. Here I thought you exaggerated your mother's lack of parental skills. I suppose you never watched *The Love Boat* or *The Ghost and Mrs. Muir* either."

"No," I said. "What's that got to do with anything?"

Before she could answer, thirsty customers called her away. I sipped my wine and thought about what she'd said. Was I jumping to conclusions? Maybe there was a simple explanation for what I'd seen.

Fatigue hit me and I wanted nothing more than to curl up at home with a cup of tea. Maybe I'd go to bed early. Setting some bills on the counter, I called to Irma and waved goodbye.

Stepping outside into the cool night, I stared up at the dark sky filled with stars and the thin sliver of the moon. I appreciated the limited streetlamps in our town that allowed us such a clear view of the night sky, but walking in near darkness made me edgy.

The sound of footsteps behind me made my heart beat even faster. As I picked up my pace, so did the footsteps. Just as I was about to make a run for home, I heard my name.

I turned to see Sandra coming toward me and stopped, relieved I wasn't being followed by someone nefarious.

"I thought that was you," she said. "Out for a walk?"

"Yes. Do you live in Serenity Cove, too?"

She shook her head. "Just went for a drive and ended up here. It's such a beautiful town."

Her hair wasn't draped over her face as it had been the last time I'd seen her. It was hard to tell in the dim light, but her cheek near her eye looked bruised.

"Is everything all right?" I asked. When she didn't answer, I added, "If you ever want to talk…"

She smiled bravely, or at least that's how it looked to me. "I'm fine, April. I'd better get home before—" She didn't finish her sentence. "There's my car. Have a good night."

She got into her car and drove away while I stood wondering what secrets Sandra was keeping from the world.

CHAPTER 8

*a*fter getting ready for art class, I came downstairs and grabbed my purse, jacket, and keys.

"You're pretty dressed up for painting," Jennifer said.

"Oh, this old thing?" I did my best to pretend I hadn't carefully chosen my outfit to fit in with Cheryl and her gang. Jennifer wasn't buying it. "I just felt like a frump last week in my old clothes."

"I don't remember the last time I saw you in heels," she said.

"They're low heels," I said, not sure why I felt defensive. "Hardly heels at all."

She smiled. "Peer pressure is a terrible thing. If they try to get you to smoke cigarettes or cut class, just say no."

"Okay, Nancy Reagan," I said, but Jennifer didn't get the reference. "You can look it up. I'm going to be late if I don't get going."

Traffic was smooth until I approached Somerton, and then it was stop and go for several miles. I made it to the community center just as class was supposed to start, so I walked as quickly as I could, regretting my choice of footwear.

I burst through the door out of breath, and everyone stopped and turned to look at me. Ron, the instructor, waited for me to settle in at my easel, then continued speaking.

"I get the feeling some of you aren't taking this class very seriously," he said, and I could have sworn his gaze lingered on Cheryl. "So, this evening, we're going to do something a little different. We're each going to paint a color wheel that we'll be able to use for reference in the future. How does that sound?"

The less than enthusiastic response from the class didn't disappoint Ron. I got the feeling he expected it. It seemed like a great exercise to me, but I didn't want anyone to think I was trying to be the teacher's pet.

As I began working on my color wheel, I glanced around the room. Cheryl and Debbie were in their usual spots, but Sandra seemed to be missing. At the break, I joined the two women. They obviously weren't all that interested in the project.

"Your color wheel's not bad," Debbie said with a shrug. "I guess I'm just not as artistic as you are."

I wanted to tell her that at least I'd made an effort, but I had something else on my mind. "Where's Sandra?" I asked Cheryl. "Is she not feeling well?"

Cheryl glanced at Debbie before answering in a whisper. "Her husband didn't come home Sunday night. He had a meeting with a business associate Sunday morning and hasn't been seen since."

"What?" I gasped. "He's been missing for two days?"

"Shhh," Debbie hissed. "We don't want people to gossip."

That seemed an odd concern to me. "You can hardly keep it a secret for long. What about his job. Isn't he an executive or something?"

"Yes," Cheryl said. "He's a VP of my father's company. Sandra's been calling in sick for him, but she'll have to tell them the truth if he stays away much longer. It's just so irresponsible."

"Irresponsible?" I didn't understand Cheryl at all. "Aren't you worried about him? Wait." A thought jumped into my mind unbidden. Whatever had fallen from that plane, it had happened on Sunday. "When did you say he went missing?"

"The last time Sandra saw him was Sunday morning before she joined us for brunch. She arrived at the restaurant at ten-thirty, I think. It was around ten-thirty, wasn't it, Deb?"

"What?" Deb's attention seemed to have wandered. "Yes, you and I got there at ten-twenty. I remember because they made a big fuss about holding the table for us. Sandra arrived five or ten minutes later."

"I see." I couldn't help but wonder if the object I'd seen falling from the plane on Sunday morning had been Sandra's husband.

"What is it?" Debbie must have noticed my concerned expression. Should I tell them my suspicions? I didn't have a shred of proof.

47

"Isn't Sandra worried something bad might have happened to him?" I asked.

Cheryl took a step closer, and her expensive perfume enveloped me. She lowered her voice. "He was a drinker. He's been known to go on benders, sometimes for days. He'll turn up."

"Oh, okay," I whispered back, but something told me he wouldn't turn up anytime soon. Not alive, at least. As quietly as I could, I told Cheryl, "But you should know something." I told her about the plane I'd seen and the thing that dropped from it. "It looked very much like a body."

Her eyes widened. "But why would Eric be on a plane?" She thought for a moment. "Maybe he went up with one of his buddies and he was so drunk he fell out."

"You think he fell out of a plane? If he was that drunk, what was he doing up in a plane?"

She shrugged. "No idea."

"And if he was alive and conscious when he fell, you'd think he'd be waving his arms and screaming or something, wouldn't you?"

She dropped her eyes to the floor, then met my eyes again. "You think it was foul play, don't you?"

"I do," I admitted.

"I've heard from my husband you've gotten yourself involved in murder investigations. He says you have surprisingly good instincts for a civilian."

"He said that?"

"When he first told me about you, I admit I was a

little jealous," she said. "But now I know I have no reason to be jealous."

"Um…" Had she just insulted me?

"Have you shared your suspicions with the police?" she asked. "If not, I can mention it to my husband."

"That would be great," I said. "I told Deputy Molina. He's the acting police chief for Serenity Cove."

"Oh, that's right. Your little town is too small for its own police force. Well, I suppose Deputy Molina is competent or they wouldn't have given him the job."

I had my own feelings on the subject, but I kept them to myself.

"Come out for a drink with me after class. We really haven't had much of a chance to get to know each other."

"Maybe next time." The break ended and I went back to my painting. As soon as class ended, I slipped out to my car before anyone noticed.

ON WEDNESDAY MORNING, Irma wanted to walk to the south end of the shore. Since that would mean we ended up at the hotel, I suspected she wanted another mimosa. I suggested we walk in the other direction.

"You always get moody and maudlin when you see the lighthouse," she complained as we trudged in the soft sand. "Then you're all quiet for the walk back."

"I just have to get used to seeing it again," I said. "You know, make new memories. Happy memories."

"Okay, we'll do a little dance when we get there. How's that?"

I laughed as she took off at full speed. As I hurried to catch up, I called out after her. "A jig? Or a tap dance? I might remember one or two steps from tap class. I only went three weeks because my mom ran behind on the fees. It was pretty embarrassing. Come to think of it, no tap dancing, okay?"

She stopped and stared at me. "What are you going on about?"

"You said we'd do a dance at the lighthouse. I just wondered what kind of dance. I've been practicing my kicks."

She shook her head and kept walking. "April May, you are one of a kind."

"That's a good thing, right?" I asked hopefully, but she didn't answer. "I just wanted to make some new happy memories," I grumbled.

By the time we reached the lighthouse, I was out of breath. I knew the boulders along the shore would be a good spot for a rest, even if the area did bring back tragic memories. I picked some wildflowers along the path and carried them with me.

As I climbed from boulder to boulder looking for a nice flat one to sit on, I paused to take in the sight of the gentle waves caressing the rocks below. I tossed the flowers as far as I could, and they floated on the wind until they landed on the shore below.

"You have five minutes for your break, and then I'm leaving with or without you," she said. She began to pace, probably wanting to keep her heart rate elevated to maintain the aerobic benefit. She stopped pacing and frowned. "What's that?"

"Huh?"

She pointed at the shore twenty or thirty feet below us. "That!"

My heart began beating wildly the moment I spotted the shape, five or six feet long. "That's whatever they dropped from the plane. I'm sure of it." I scrambled to my feet and began making my way down the boulder-strewn slope.

"Wait," Irma called after me. "Shouldn't we call the police?"

I stopped. "I suppose so. You call and I'll check out what it is."

"Wait," she called out again, but this time I ignored her. I made my way slowly down the rocky terrain, which wasn't easy. The slope finally flattened out and I found myself on a pebbly beach. I grabbed a piece of driftwood a couple of feet long and approached the lumpy, brown shape.

Irma's voice behind me called, "Molina is on his way. He told us to wait and not to touch it."

"Like with our hands?" I asked. I didn't plan to touch it—just give it a few pokes. As I walked closer, I knew that I wouldn't have to touch or poke it to know what it was. I held my breath, not wanting to accept the truth.

"Is that a shoe?" Irma asked.

"Yes," I said, letting out my breath. "It's attached to a foot. Which is attached to a body. A very dead body."

CHAPTER 9

*I*rma made a second call to Molina, this time to let him know what he would find on his arrival.

"What did he say?" I asked.

"First he said, 'You're kidding,' and then there were some expletives that I won't repeat. Then something about 'that bleeping April May,' only he didn't use the word 'bleeping,' if you know what I mean."

"Yes, I think I do, though I'm not sure why he's mad at me for being right." I almost added, "again," but I didn't want to overdo it. "That body must be what I saw fall from the plane on Sunday."

"So much for the happy memories," Irma said. "I guess we'll be walking to the hotel from now on. After Molina gets here, want to go have some eggs Benedict?"

I shook my head. "I'm not hungry."

"Me neither, but I wouldn't say no to a mimosa. Or

maybe a shot of whiskey. Just to calm my nerves, of course."

I sat on a nearby boulder and Irma paced while we waited in silence. Someone called out and I looked up at the top of the cliff where Molina looked down at us. I waved.

Molina slowly made his way to us, but before he arrived, I wanted to ask Irma one question.

"Any idea who he is?" I asked.

"That's Molina," she said. "Do you need to get your eyes checked?"

"Not him," I huffed. "The dead man."

"None." She glanced at the body but didn't go any closer.

I didn't blame her. I'd gotten as close to the man as I wanted to. At least, I assumed it was a man based on his clothes and hairstyle. Also, from what I could tell, he had the build of a man, but who knew what three days in the ocean would do to one's figure.

Molina's greeting came out in a grunt as he slipped on the uneven terrain and had to swing his arms to keep from falling. He composed himself and headed towards me first.

He scowled at me before turning to Irma. "I understand you called in a 419." When she responded with raised eyebrows, he clarified, "A dead body." Before she could answer, he walked toward the body. Small waves crashed over it as the tide receded, and the deputy gingerly waded closer as he pulled on gloves.

His phone rang and he gave someone directions.

Soon two officers appeared and made their way down the cliffside.

"Probably reinforcements from the sheriff's office," I told Irma.

The two young officers, one male and one female, passed us, the woman nodding at us in acknowledgment. They reached Molina, and the three of them dragged the body away from the water. Molina searched his pockets.

The county coroner, Dr. Fredeline Severs, arrived next. Freddie, as her friends called her, clambered down the hillside. She said a quick "Hello, ladies," before joining the officers.

While she began her examination, Molina walked over to us, the two officers following him.

Before he could say anything, I had a question. "Is that who was pushed out of the plane on Sunday? Can you tell how long he was in the water?"

"I'll ask the questions, Ms. May, if you don't mind."

Oh, that's how we were going to play it. "Of course, Deputy Molina," I said in my most ingratiating voice. "I just thought that if Mr. Vitello's body had been pushed out of the plane on Sunday, that might help you pinpoint time of death, not to mention give you some clues about his murderer. But please, proceed with your questions."

"How did you know that"—he jerked his head in the direction of the shore—"was Eric Vitello?"

"I didn't," I said. "But now I do."

I stood and brushed the sand off my pants. "If you'd

like to question Ms. Vargas or myself, we will be at my tearoom having a stiff drink to recover from our shock."

Without waiting for a response from Molina, Irma and I scaled the hill and headed home.

IRMA and I climbed my front steps, and I unlocked the front door. I didn't expect Jennifer to be home, but I called out her name just to make sure. Irma followed me to the kitchen where I put on a pot of coffee and pulled a bottle of whiskey down from an upper cabinet.

"Do you want the whiskey in the coffee or straight?" I asked. "I'm making an Irish coffee and I can make one for you, too." I returned from the refrigerator with a jug of cream. "I forgot. You're probably not supposed to have cream, are you?"

"Just pour me a shot," she said, and I obliged.

I decided to have cookies with my Irish coffee. When Irma grabbed two shortbread cookies, I didn't scold her. It's not every day you find a dead body.

After I poured our coffee, we retreated to the front room, sitting at the table by the front window.

"I'm glad we're not open today," I said. "It will give me a chance to think of what to say tomorrow when everyone starts asking me about finding the dead body."

"How'd you know who he was?" Irma asked.

"Sandra's husband didn't come home Sunday night,"

I explained. "She reported him missing the next morning." Doing my best to remember the events of Sunday morning, I pulled out my phone. "Cheryl texted me a little after nine o'clock and invited me to brunch. Then I got this text telling me the dolphins were running and I might be able to see them from my front porch. We'd been talking about dolphins and whales on Thursday when the girls stopped by."

Irma's eyebrows raised slightly. "The girls?"

I smiled. "That's what they call each other. I figured the text came from Bree, since she's got a thing for whales and dolphins. She's the youngest—late twenties or early thirties, I'd guess." I got up and retrieved the photos of the plane from my purse. They'd been time stamped. "I took this picture a few minutes after eleven o'clock."

"What are you getting at?" Irma asked. "Why is the timeline so important?"

"Cheryl, Debbie, and Sandra, and maybe Bree too, were at brunch together and can vouch for each other's whereabouts when Sandra's husband was pushed out of that plane."

"So?" Irma asked.

"You know how when someone is killed, they say it's almost always the spouse?" I asked. "Sandra has an alibi. Which is very lucky for her, don't you think?"

I offered to fix lunch for Irma and me, but she had errands to run. I made myself a sandwich and a glass of iced tea and sat at the kitchen island to eat.

Chef Emile watched me from the corner of the

kitchen for some time before he spoke. "There is something that bothers you, *non?*"

"Yes," I said, staring at my empty plate, not remembering eating my lunch. "A body. There's been another murder."

"*Zut alors!*" he said. "You must stop this finding of dead bodies. It is not good for your digestion."

Turning to him wide-eyed, I repeated, "Digestion?"

"*Mais oui,*" he said. "A calm and relaxed demeanor is most important to stimulate the gastric juices that assist in the absorption of the nutrients into the system."

"Is that so," I said nearly laughing at his description. "I'll have you know, I don't go out looking for dead bodies. If I had my way, I'd never find another one as long as I lived. It's no fun, you know, and neither is being accused of murder or having to visit your friends in jail."

The buzzing of my phone interrupted my rant. Looking at the screen, I groaned.

"What is it, *ma chère?*" Chef asked.

"My brother, Jeff. He's in San Francisco and he wants to visit tomorrow and stay for a few days."

"And this is bad?"

"No," I said as a pang of guilt stabbed me in the chest. My brother was the only family I had. Maybe he'd gotten over his anger and resentment. "It's just… complicated."

"I see," Chef said, but I wasn't at all sure he did. "So will he be coming here to this house?"

"Yes." I texted Jeff a reply that I would love to see

him. I even put an exclamation point at the end to indicate my sincerity. A response came back within seconds, and I felt my jaw drop as I read it.

"What is it?" Chef asked.

"He's coming with his wife." I looked up into Chef's questioning face. "I didn't even know he was married!"

CHAPTER 10

I spent the rest of Wednesday cleaning the upper floor, scrubbing floors, dusting, and doing all those tasks I'd put off. Then I stood at the door of the guest room and took in the faded bedspread and ancient carpets. I'd never gotten around to redoing this room and it was just the way it was when I'd moved in, but a little less dusty. Besides the fact that the room looked tired and dismal, the old sheets and towels wouldn't do for my brother and especially his new wife, who I knew nothing about. I made a plan to drive to one of the department stores in Somerton the next morning.

After a fitful night, I awoke to gray skies, which didn't improve my mood. My anxiety grew with every thought. Why was my brother coming to visit? Would he want to dig up past grievances? Would his new wife like me? After a quick shower, I found Jennifer in the kitchen and filled her in on my news, nearly yelling over the sound of the cappuccino maker.

"I can stay with my grandma while they're here," she said.

"You don't have to do that," I assured her.

"It's okay. Actually," she paused and gave me a hopeful smile. "I was planning to ask you if you would mind if I moved out. My grandmother wants me to come live with her. She gets lonely."

"Of course, I don't mind. I'll miss having you around all the time, but I'll still get to see plenty of you. I think it's great that you're making up for lost time."

She set the cappuccino in front of me and gave me a hug. "You're the best."

"I guess I'll really have to learn how to use the espresso machine now. Do you want to drive to Somerton with me to do some shopping this morning? I want to get new sheets and towels for the guest room. And a new comforter."

"I think I'll stay here and start prepping for today," she said. "That way you won't have to rush back."

After spending an excessive amount on designer sheets, comforters, drapes, towels, and fancy soaps, I returned in time to help Jennifer finish prepping for the day.

"What would I do without you?" I asked when I realized there was little left for me to do.

While I threw the new sheets in the washer with a cup of baking soda to soften them up, the thought popped into my mind that she'd find another job one day, certainly when she finished college. I'd have to plan for the inevitable, although I couldn't imagine replacing her. I put the sad thought out of my mind.

The rest of the day flew by as I went from baking and preparing tea trays to getting the guest room ready with all my purchases. I'd gone with an understated yet classic look with soft blues and whites, and when I'd finished, I stood back and admired my work. Hopefully it would meet the new Mrs. May's approval.

After scrubbing down every surface until it gleamed, I rearranged the guest bathroom. I laid out fresh, fluffy towels and a basket of everything a guest might need—lotion, shampoo and conditioner, toothpaste and toothbrushes. It was important to me that they felt welcome and at home. Besides, our little town didn't have a 24-hour quick-mart if they forgot any essentials.

Back downstairs, I double checked that everything was ready. I had defrosted enough beef bourguignon to feed a family of six and made sure there was plenty of fresh bread.

"Ah," Chef commented as he watched me in my preparations. "An excellent choice."

"I hope so," I said. "I've yet to meet anyone who didn't love my, I mean *your*, beef bourguignon." After all, it was Chef's recipe, and I might as well give him credit before he corrected me. "I want to make a good impression." A thought popped into my head. "But what if his wife is vegan?" I began to panic. "Why didn't I think of possible dietary issues sooner?"

"Vegan?" Chef's eyebrows drew together. "What is this word?"

"It's like vegetarian. You've heard of that right?" When Chef answered with a curt nod, I added, "Vegans don't eat any kind of animal products, like butter, milk, or eggs." I pulled out the recipe for parsnip and carrot soup. Of course, it called for milk, and it wouldn't be the same without it.

Grabbing one of Chef's cookbooks, I flipped the pages. Maybe a salad? I read through the ingredients, but nearly every one listed cheese, eggs, or even bacon.

Years ago, I'd attended a meditation retreat where they served meatless dishes, one of which I'd recreated. I found a similar recipe online. Vegan chickpea stew had no meat, dairy, or eggs, and it was gluten-free. I recalled buying the ingredients, intending to make it again, and never getting around to it.

One of the best things about the recipe, is that nearly all the ingredients were non-perishable. The only exception was lime juice, but I nearly always had a lime or two on hand. After quickly checking that I had everything I needed, I got to work.

The recipe took less than an hour from start to finish. After sautéing sliced red onions in coconut oil along with garlic and ginger, I added the spices to toast them. Chef had once explained that this technique would release the flavors, though I doubted he'd ever cooked with garam masala.

Next, I added the diced tomatoes and let them cook for several minutes before adding the coconut milk and chickpeas. After simmering for ten minutes or so, I added the last ingredient—fresh lime juice. I turned off the burner and tasted the final product. The mixture of flavors woke up my tastebuds, and I remembered why I liked the dish so much.

If I didn't serve the curry tonight, I knew it would taste even better the next day, like so many flavorful soups and stews. There were many reasons leftovers tasted even better when reheated a day or two later—excess water soaks into the dish's starch, and proteins break down and release amino acids which enhance the savory or umami tastes.

As I put the lid on the pan to keep the curry warm, my phone rang. I answered, hearing my brother's voice at the other end.

"Hi Jeff," I said as cheerfully as I could muster considering my anxiety. "Are you on your way?"

"We're here. At the hotel." He paused. "I thought we'd check in and get settled, but they need a credit card number before they'll give us a room."

"Uh-huh." I wasn't sure why he was telling me this. Wasn't that how all hotels worked?

"So, if I give the phone to the front desk guy, would you give him that information?"

"What information?" I asked.

I heard the sigh through the phone. "Your credit card number."

During the moment or two of silence it dawned on me. He expected me to pay to put him and his new wife up at the hotel.

My shoulder muscles tensed. "But I have everything ready for you here—new sheets and towels and all that. I thought you two would stay with me. It's a big house."

"Oh." His voice told me he didn't care for the idea. "It's just that I think Lulu would be more comfortable at the hotel."

"Lulu?" For a moment I thought he had brought a dog along. "Oh—is Lulu your new wife's name?"

Another sigh. "Who else would I be talking about? Can I hand the phone to the front desk guy now?"

I felt my resolve deflate. "Sure. Will the two of you at least come over for dinner?"

"Lulu is just exhausted," he said. "We'll get an early dinner here. Why don't you stop by for a drink later?"

I had a better idea. "The Mermaid Cafe is a short walk from the hotel. Why don't I meet you there at say, seven-thirty?" When I didn't get an immediate answer, I added, "They carry Courvoisier. I remember that was your favorite. Is it still?"

"I suppose we can meet you there," he said.

"I can't wait to meet Lulu," I said, but he'd already handed the phone to the front desk agent.

I SAT at the kitchen island, my chin in my hands. I'd wanted everything to be perfect for Jeff's visit, and he'd ruined it before I even saw him. Or was it my idealized idea of a brother-sister relationship that was the problem?

Jennifer came down the back staircase with a duffle bag over her shoulder. "Are your brother and his wife on their way?" When she saw the look on my face, she asked, "What's wrong? Are they not coming?"

"They're staying at the hotel."

"After everything you did to get ready for them?

The new comforter and everything else? That's disappointing."

I shrugged. "I should know better than to expect Jeff to be any different than he's always been. I guess I just thought since he had a new wife…"

"Has he been married before?" Jennifer asked.

"No, never." I got up and poured myself a cup of tea and heated it up in the microwave. "Don't tell anyone you saw me do that. My reputation as the town's tea snob would be ruined."

She chuckled. "My lips are sealed."

Back on my stool, I wrapped my hands around the now warm cup. "I figured he just wasn't the settling down type. My mom never stopped hoping, though. She really wanted grandchildren."

"Do you think he'll have kids now that he's married?"

I nearly spit out my tea. "At his age?"

"What age is that?"

"Let's see." I did the addition in my head. "He just turned sixty-three. He's nearly thirteen years older than me, which I always figured was why we weren't close. He mostly lived with his dad, and he'd moved out on his own by the time I was in kindergarten."

Jennifer put down her bag and joined me at the island. "Want me to stay and keep you company this evening?"

"Nah, I'm fine. I'm meeting them at the Mermaid Cafe in a little while. But you don't have to stay with your grandmother since they'll be at the hotel."

She put an arm around my shoulder and gave me a

squeeze. "Maybe they'll change their minds and stay here tomorrow night after they see the place. It's way nicer than the hotel."

"That's true," I said, her words reviving me. "They don't know what they're missing."

After Jennifer left, I nibbled at leftover scones and stared at the picture of the plane. I wished I'd held the camera steadier so I could make out the identification numbers painted on the side.

Remembering that Molina had called them "N-numbers," I did an internet search and found the FAA's website where I could enter an "N-number" and retrieve ownership information. After trying several possible combinations, I gave up.

Molina must not have gotten anywhere with the photo either, or I would have heard from him. But would he have let me know? He never liked me getting involved in what he considered "his" investigations. I called and left him a message anyway.

Maybe if I put the picture on social media, someone could identify it. I paused, thinking Molina might disapprove, but I went ahead and did it anyway. I uploaded the picture, captioning it "Something fell from this plane—can anyone help me solve the mystery?" Then I added several hashtags hoping they would help the post get noticed.

I glanced at the clock and jumped off my stool. I'd have to hurry, or I'd be late. I grabbed my purse and jacket. I stepped outside and returned for my keys. It would be quicker to drive.

Stepping inside the Mermaid Cafe, I felt my anxiety

diminish. The colors and lights had a soothing effect along with the sound of gently crashing waves. I never knew if Irma played a recording or just put a microphone at the back of the restaurant where the ocean met the shore.

A big part of the reason I wanted my brother and Lulu to meet us here was so I'd have Irma for moral support. I'd texted her earlier to let her know what to expect. Not that I was all that sure I knew what to expect.

As soon as my eyes adjusted to the dim light, I scanned the room for Jeff and his wife, but it appeared they hadn't arrived yet. I headed for the bar and perched on a stool waiting for Irma to finish serving drinks and notice me. She soon headed my way.

She leaned her bony elbows on the bar and said, "You look as anxious as a fish that just realized his dinner has a hook in it." She pushed herself up and poured me a whiskey on the rocks. "Here. I'm sure everything will be just fine."

"What if Lulu doesn't like me?" I asked. "That's his new wife's name."

Irma put her hands on her hips. "If she doesn't love you the way all of us do, then that's her loss. You can't make other people's minds up for them, you know."

I took a swallow of my drink while I thought that over. "I suppose you're right."

Patting my hand, she said, "I bet the two of you will be fast friends." She gestured behind me. "Looks like they're here."

I swung around on my stool. My brother hadn't

changed much—maybe a little gray in his hair and thickness around the middle, but still handsome in a worn-out sort of way. He whispered something in the ear of the woman next to him and then he and I made eye contact.

Jeff and Lulu made their way over to me, and I did my best to relax or at least appear that way.

"Hey, sis." He gave me a brief hug.

When he stepped back, I waited to be introduced to his wife, but after several seconds of awkward silence, I said, "You must be Lulu."

Lulu broke into a wide grin. "Yes, I am, ma'am." I detected a slight southern accent, or perhaps she hailed from the Midwest.

"Please, call me April." I stepped closer and whispered, "Can I give you a hug?"

That was all the prompting she needed. She threw her arms around me and held me tightly before letting me go.

"It's so nice to meet you, ma'am—I mean, April."

"I'm glad you could come out for a drink," I said. "I'm sure you're tired from traveling."

"Oh, no," she said. "It was an easy drive from San Francisco. That's where we spent our honeymoon. When Jeff told me we were coming to see you, his only family, I couldn't wait to meet you."

Jeff ordered a Courvoisier for himself, and a lemon drop for Lulu. He pulled out two stools, arranging to sit between Lulu and me. If he didn't want us getting too chummy, his plan backfired.

I leaned forward on the bar so I could talk with

Lulu, not letting him come between me and my new sister-in-law. "Lulu is such a cute name. Is it short for something?"

Her cheeks reddened. "My name is Louise, but Jeff started calling me Lulu the first time we met." She set her gaze on him. "It was love at first sight, wasn't it, Jeff?"

Jeff took her hand in his. "It sure was."

"I didn't even know Jeff was dating someone," I said, taking another swig of whiskey. "How did you meet?"

Lulu glanced at Jeff before answering. "It was at a country-western bar in Fresno. I worked part-time there as a cocktail waitress. I'm a pre-school teacher, but it doesn't pay much, and besides, I liked working at the Wild Horse Saloon."

"You're a country music fan?" I asked. I had nothing against country music, I'd just never been exposed to it much.

"Sure am. And I love dancing, too." She leaned closer, and Jeff pulled back, possibly regretting sitting between us. "So, one night, as I was serving drinks, this tall, handsome stranger," she nodded in Jeff's direction, "asked me if he could take me to dinner. And three weeks later, we were married!"

I nearly fell off my stool "Three weeks?" I tried to keep the shock from showing on my face, plastering on a smile instead. "That's fast. I guess it really was love at first sight."

"Sure was," Lulu said, and took a sip of her lemon drop. "My, that's delicious. Do you think the lady bartender would give me her recipe?"

Jeff snorted. "Someone should tell her the wig isn't fooling anyone. What is she, eighty?"

Lulu grimaced for a split second, a seemingly involuntary reaction to Jeff's insult. Irma chose that moment to reappear before us.

"Are you enjoying your drinks?" she asked.

"Oh, yes," Lulu gushed. "This lemon drop is simply delish."

"Irma, I'd like you to meet my brother, Jeff," I turned to my brother. "This is my good friend Irma Vargas."

He pretended as if he hadn't just insulted her. "Nice to meet you."

"And this is his wife, Lulu."

Lulu grinned. "We're newlyweds. Jeff got me this cute little ring." She held out her left hand. "It's just temporary, but isn't it adorable?"

I reached in front of Jeff to take her hand and get a look of the little ring. It had tiny stones in the shape of ladybugs.

"I just love ladybugs, don't you?" Lulu asked, not waiting for an answer. "They're good luck, you know."

"It's lovely," I said sincerely. I'd never seen any correlation between the size of the diamonds on a ring and the success of a relationship. "But you said it's temporary. Have you not decided on a permanent one yet?"

"Well, you see," Lulu began, "Jeff has promised me a big diamond as soon as—"

"Let's go, Lulu," Jeff said, pushing his chair back with a loud scrape. "I know you're tired from the long drive."

"Oh," Lulu's face fell. "Well, I suppose I am. I guess I was so excited to meet your sister I forgot all about it." She slid off her stool. "I'm so glad I got to meet you, April."

Jeff patted my arm. "We'll talk tomorrow."

"Come for lunch or tea any time after noon. I'd love for both of you to see the house."

"We'll see." Jeff took Lulu's hand, clearly wanting to leave.

Lulu didn't take the hint, instead throwing her arms around me. She whispered in my ear. "I've never had a sister. I hope we can be very good friends."

"Let's go, Lulu." Jeff's impatience slipped into his voice.

"I'm coming," she answered. "Hold your horses."

After watching them leave, I turned back around on my stool to find Irma staring at me.

"So that's your brother," she said.

"What is that supposed to mean?" I asked.

She chuckled. "Let's just say I fully understand why the two of you aren't close. I suppose it's nice he came to town so you could meet Lulu."

"Yeah," I agreed. "But I get a feeling that's not the real reason he's here."

CHAPTER 11

Friday morning, I took another inventory of supplies to make sure we'd make it through the weekend. If we had another warm weekend like the previous one, we'd need to be prepared. I had a freezer full of soups and stews, but they weren't especially popular on sunny days.

I hadn't made full-sized quiches in a while. A slice of quiche along with a Caesar salad had proved very popular over the summer.

We were low on eggs, so Jennifer volunteered to make a trip to the grocery store. By the time she left, her list included cucumbers, dill, and heavy cream. She stopped by Molly's bakery on the way back for fresh thin-sliced bread.

I left Jeff a message asking what time he and Lulu planned to stop by, but didn't get a response. I felt let down and disappointed, but why did I think Jeff would be excited to see what I'd achieved? He'd never been interested in my career before.

Jennifer sat at the island with her café mocha. "Your coffee is getting cold. Why don't you sit down for a minute and tell me about your new sister-in-law?"

I plopped down at the island across from her. "I invited them to come in for lunch today. Lulu seems really sweet. It's just... I don't know. Something feels off."

"Like what?" she asked.

I thought for a moment, trying to put my finger on what niggled at my brain. "For one thing, she has this cute little wedding band, but then she said that it was only temporary. I got the feeling that Jeff promised her a big diamond."

"What's wrong with that?" she asked. "Maybe he's saving up."

I shook my head. "She said something like 'he promised me a big diamond as soon as—,' but he didn't let her finish her sentence."

Jennifer gave me a maternal look as if she were the mature, experienced one. "There could be any number of reasons why he didn't want her telling you all their business. Not everyone wants their family to know their secrets."

She had a point. "I suppose you're right. I've gotten so used to looking for clues, I've started seeing them everywhere. Speaking of clues..." I pulled out my phone and checked if anyone had commented on the picture I'd posted on social media. "There's only one comment on the picture I posted of the plane, and it's just a picture of another plane."

Jennifer put her dishes in the dishwasher and began

setting up for the day. She liked to bundle napkins and silverware first thing. After that, she'd usually start slicing cucumbers. She had once told me that she found routine comforting. I found it deadly boring, so I tended to do things in a different order each day. Sometimes it got me in trouble, but Jennifer often saved the day when I forgot something important.

I compared the picture that a user posted in their comment to my photo. My heart beat a little faster when I realized they might be the same plane. The time stamp on the photo convinced me.

And I could make out every letter and number on the side of the plane.

"I'll be right back," I said to Jennifer and hurried to my office upstairs. Opening the FAA website, I put in the n-number of the plane in the new photo. I held my breath and hit enter.

The answer came back: The number was deregistered. The manufacturer name and model were listed but the cancel date showed November of 1988. That made no sense.

Scrolling down, it showed the previous registration, but under name and address it said "none."

I double checked the photo to make sure the numbers were right. Whoever had posted it had taken a crystal-clear photo and there was no mistaking the numbers. Before I gave up on the idea, I sent a message to the commenter—username "justplanefacts319" asking if he knew why a plane with a deregistered n-number was flying around our area.

Then I called Deputy Molina and left him a message with the new information and photo.

"That's all I can do for now," I told myself. "I have a tearoom to run."

～

AROUND TWO IN THE AFTERNOON, Jennifer returned to the kitchen after serving a tiered tray of afternoon tea treats.

"I thought you said your brother and his wife were stopping by for lunch today," she commented as she readied another tray.

"I said I'd invited him. He didn't seem to want to commit. Why did they come to Serenity Cove if they didn't want to spend time with me?"

Jennifer stopped what she was doing and turned to me. "I'm sure they'll stop by later. How long are they staying?"

"He didn't say. Although with me footing the bill at the hotel, he won't be in any hurry to leave."

She frowned. "I always like to give people the benefit of the doubt, but I don't think I like your brother very much."

"Wait until you meet him before you make your final judgment." My brother could charm almost anyone when he wanted to. Would he even bother with Jennifer since she was only my assistant? Maybe, if only because she was young and pretty.

I shook off the thought, not wanting to get frustrated over nothing. Before I let my temper get the better of me, I'd have to wait and see what happened.

I didn't have to wait long.

~

JENNIFER STUCK her head in the kitchen door. "Someone's here to see you." Before I could ask who, she slipped back into the tearoom.

I pulled my apron off over my head and took a quick look at my reflection in the toaster, tucking an unruly strand of hair behind my ear. I pushed the door open and stepped into the tearoom.

Lulu stood near the front door examining a display of items for sale. She picked up a flowered tea towel, glancing at the price before setting it back down.

I called out a welcome as I approached. "I'm so glad you could come," I said sincerely, taking her by both her hands giving them a squeeze before letting them go. She wore a flowered skirt and a peach-toned sweater set. "You look lovely, by the way."

"So do you," she said, then gazing around the room, added, "This place is beautiful. Did you do all the decorating yourself?"

"Jennifer helped a lot. She's my assistant who greeted you." I paused and we stood awkwardly for a moment, neither knowing what to say. "Is Jeff coming?"

"No," she said. "Um, he had to do something. Work. He had to work."

"That's okay." I hid my disappointment. "That will give us time to get to know each other."

She grinned and reached out for a hug. When she let go, she said, "That's what I'd hoped."

"Would you like me to show you around the house? Have you eaten? Would you like something to eat first?"

She shook her head. "I'm not hungry. I'd love a tour of your house."

"Great. We'll start with the downstairs." I spoke softly so I didn't disturb the few diners who lingered, finishing their desserts. "Long ago, most of the first-floor walls were removed to open up the space for a restaurant. I didn't have to do much to turn it into a tearoom—just some redecorating." I led her to the study. "Now, this room, we completely renovated to make it fitting for special events. I wanted it to have a more masculine vibe but feel comfortable and welcoming to everyone. Some men aren't particularly comfortable around flowered tablecloths and delicate china."

She stepped inside the room and took in the huge bookcases, paneling, and heavy red velour drapes. "Oh, my. It's like stepping back in time."

I nearly had to drag her out of the room. "I've got lots more to show you."

We stepped into the kitchen. Jennifer looked up with a smile and I introduced them officially, partly for Chef's benefit since he watched from a corner of the room.

"There are two sets of stairs," I explained, gesturing to the stairway that led upstairs from the kitchen.

We climbed the narrow rear staircase to the second-floor hallway. "The house was originally built as two separate residences, so there's actually a kitchen up here too, but we hardly use it." I pointed to the kitchen door.

Lulu stepped inside and took a quick look. "It's almost identical to the downstairs kitchen."

"I think both floors were nearly identical before they remodeled downstairs. There's one bathroom back there," I gestured to a door, "with an old clawfoot tub."

Her face lit up. "This I gotta see." She stepped into the bathroom. "It looks like you've hardly changed a thing."

I stood in the doorway. "I haven't gotten around to fixing it up, but I'm planning to keep the tile floors and especially the tub."

"Oh, yes." She took one more look before joining me in the hallway. "What's that door?"

"That goes to the attic." I was about to walk past the door when I stopped and asked, "Would you like to meet Whisk? I have no idea if he's feeling sociable today, but we can see."

"Whisk?"

I grinned. "The house came with a Bengal cat who'd been living in the attic for months or maybe longer. He's skittish around people, but he seems to be getting used to me."

"I'd love to meet him," Lulu said.

We climbed the stairs and stepped into the cluttered attic. "Watch your step. We haven't had a chance to reinforce the floors yet." I pointed to Whisk's favorite chair. "Have a seat if you don't mind getting cat hair on your clothes."

"I don't mind at all," she said. "I asked Jeff if we could get a cat. Or a dog. I think he wants us to get settled in before we add to our family." At that she blushed, which made me wonder if they planned to have children.

I clicked my tongue and called Whisk's name. "Hey, boy. I brought someone for you to meet."

Lulu and I both turned at the pitter patter of paws, and Whisk appeared at the top of a bookcase. He surveyed both of us suspiciously. At least, that's how I interpreted his expression.

He made a sound something between a purr and a roar followed by a "wrahw."

"Oh, my," Lulu said softly. "Aren't you beautiful! Would you like to come sit on my lap? I'm very good at scratching kitty ears." When Whisk gave her a meow that sounded more like "mrahw?" she said, as if answering him, "Oh, yes. I understand. My name's Lulu, and I love pretty kitties like you. I'd like to be your friend if that's all right with you."

Whisk leapt off the bookcase, landing effortlessly on a box. Then, to my surprise, he sauntered over to Lulu and jumped on her lap. As she scratched his ears as promised, he kneaded her lap, purring loudly.

"Don't his claws hurt?" I asked.

"A little," she admitted, "but I don't mind." She

added in a baby-girl voice, "You're a sweet boy, aren't you Whisk?"

A noise from somewhere outside caught the cat's attention and he pushed off Lulu's lap hard and ran off.

"Oof!" she put her hand to her chest. "That startled me."

"He has the run of the neighborhood," I explained. "I know it's not ideal, but he's been on his own so long, I haven't been able to change his habits."

Once Lulu accepted that Whisk wasn't returning anytime soon, we made our way back to the second floor. I led her to the upstairs parlor at the front of the house.

"I use this as my office and TV room," I said. "Although during the day, the view is a distraction."

Lulu moved to the window and stared at the ocean. "It's so lovely, April. You're so lucky to live here."

"And I know it, believe me." We stepped back into the hall, and I pointed out the door to Jennifer's bedroom. Next, I gave her a quick look at my room and led her to the newly redecorated guest bedroom.

"Oh, my," she gasped. "It's gorgeous." She stepped inside and examined the antique dresser and night-stands. "I love the colors you picked out for the comforter and the drapes. They look brand new."

"They are. I had assumed you and Jeff would stay here, so I used that as an excuse to fix up the room." When I saw the surprised look on her face, I realized Jeff had never told her I'd offered to put them up. I quickly added, "I didn't realize you two were newlyweds, so of course I understand why you'd want your privacy."

She sat on the bed and gave it a little bounce. Her ever-present smile had disappeared, replaced by an expression I couldn't quite decipher.

"You and Jeff are welcome to stay with me anytime," I said. "If not on this trip, maybe another time."

"You seem so nice," she said, still not smiling.

Her comment took me aback. I didn't know how to respond. What did she mean I "seemed" so nice?

She clutched her hands tightly in her lap and lifted her chin as if about to pick a fight. "Jeff told me about how when your mother died, that you cut him out of the inheritance." She fixed her gaze on the headboard avoiding my gaze. "He said he didn't make a big deal out of it at the time because it was just him, but now that he's married, he's decided that he wants his fair share. For us. For our future together."

"Oh." I reached for the armchair in the corner and sat down. "So that's the real reason you're here. For money. Not to see me."

Lulu said nothing, fiddling with her ladybug ring.

"Lulu, I have something to tell you, and you're probably not going to like it." Who was I kidding? She definitely wouldn't like it. "Our mother had no money of her own. About twenty years ago, when she got evicted from her apartment for not paying rent, I bought her a house. I'd been successful in my career, so I could afford it. Just barely. I made the mortgage payments and paid the property taxes, upkeep, mainte-nance, and all that until the day she died."

"But Jeff says…"

"Let me finish, please. When I'm done, I can show you all the documentation if you want. Or you can choose not to believe me. It's totally up to you. But the house my mother lived in was in my name. And when she passed away, I sold it."

"But she had a will. Jeff says she left half of everything to him, including the house, and he got almost nothing."

"That's because she owned almost nothing. He must have known that. Our mother barely managed to put food on the table when we were young, and she only got worse over time. She meant well, I really believe she did, but she never could keep a job or a husband. She had three, you know. Jeff and I have different fathers."

She stared at her hands and slowly rocked back and forth on the bed. We sat quietly for several minutes while I let my words sink in. Whether she believed me or not, I couldn't tell.

"I'm sorry," I said finally. "I would have liked for us to be friends. I've never had a sister either."

At that, she burst into tears. I sat down next to her on the bed and put my arm around her shoulders which only made her sob more loudly.

"It's okay," I murmured. "It'll be okay."

Grabbing the box of tissues on the nightstand, I handed them to her. "I'm going downstairs now. Take your time and when you're ready, I'll fix you an afternoon tea like nothing you've ever had."

"That's easy," she sniffled. "I've never had afternoon tea."

"That will never do." I patted her hand. "I'll warn you, though. Once you've had afternoon tea at SereniTea tearoom, everything else will seem like a pale imitation."

When I entered the kitchen using the back staircase, Jennifer asked, "Where's Lulu?"

I briefly told her about our conversation. "She's composing herself and then she'll come down for afternoon tea. I want to make it really special."

"Can I help?" Jennifer asked.

"Of course," I said. "But then, you help just by being here." *What would I do without you?* I added to myself as I did so often lately.

While I waited for Lulu, Jennifer readied a tiered tray for two, and I checked my messages. One came from someone named Parker who turned out to be justplanefacts139.

N# deregistered super sus, he wrote. *What info do u have?*

Not much," I messaged him in return. I didn't feel comfortable explaining that I thought that whoever had flown that plane might have been a murderer. At the very least, they must have been an accomplice.

"What does 'sus' mean?" I asked Jennifer.

She placed two mini creampuffs on the top tier of our tea tray. "It means suspicious, like when something's sort of sketchy."

"Like Irma turned down cookies. That's sus?"

She grinned. "That would be totally sus."

CHAPTER 12

*A*ll of the other diners had left, and Lulu and I sat at my favorite table in front of the window. She stared out at the sea while I filled her teacup with my favorite rose petal black tea. While I prattled on about the contents of the tea and other tea facts, she appeared to listen but didn't say a word.

All that changed when Jennifer placed an over-flowing tiered tray in the middle of the table. Lulu's eyes widened at the sight of finger sandwiches in various shapes, mini quiches, cookies, cakes, and other treats.

"Help yourself," I said. "There's two of each item, so I expect you to try everything. If there's anything you don't care for, you don't have to finish it."

"I can't imagine there's anything here that doesn't taste scrumptious." She stared at the tower of food as if not knowing where to start. I put a few sandwiches on my plate and she followed suit.

Soon, her bubbling personality returned as she

asked me about the ingredients in each sandwich and how I came up with so many wonderful recipes.

"Funny story," I said, though if I told her the real story, she'd never believe it. "A French chef named Emile Toussaint ran the kitchen here when it was a restaurant in the late fifties and early sixties. When I first moved in, I found several cookbooks he'd written. I'd done lots of baking before, but he was my introduction to French cooking. I adapted his quiche recipe, for the mini quiches. He doesn't—" I caught myself. "I mean, I don't think he would approve." Chef liked to tell me that a quiche could be cut into smaller portions and didn't seem to understand the concept of a mini quiche.

Lulu had a surprisingly good appetite for someone who was in tears not long before. Red still rimmed her eyes, but the color had come back into her cheeks.

As she stuffed a creampuff in her mouth, she glanced at her phone and nearly cried out. "I had no idea it was so late." She stood and threw her purse over her shoulder. "Jeff is asking where I am. I'm sorry to run off like this."

Before I could even stand up, she hurried to the door, stopping only to repeat, "Sorry," and "Thank you."

Feeling emotionally exhausted from my encounter with Lulu, I returned to the table by the window and poured myself another cup of tea.

Jennifer removed the other cup and dishes and insisted that I stay put. "I can finish up by myself. I can tell by the look on your face that you have a lot to process."

For someone in her early twenties, she was surprisingly wise at times. Did I have a lot to process? Or did I simply need to accept that my brother would never be anyone other than who he'd always proved himself to be?

But now Lulu was in the picture. He might be angry when she told him what I'd said. I didn't mind him being angry with me—heck, I was used to it. But I hated to think he might take it out on her. She wasn't a child, and yet she seemed so innocent.

The front door opened, and I looked up. A teenager with dark, wavy hair stepped inside. He wore baggy jeans, an oversized T-shirt on his thin frame, and a pair of high-top Converse sneakers. His pale face was thin too, with high cheekbones.

"I'm sorry, but we're closed." I often forgot to lock the front door, but the hours were plainly posted on it. Then again, he didn't look like our typical customer.

"Are you April May?" he asked.

"Yes." I stood and walked toward him. "And you are?"

"I'm Parker."

"Oh." I stopped in my tracks. I'd expected him to be older. "Nice to meet you. Have you always been interested in planes?"

"A lot more goes on up in the sky than you would think," he answered cryptically.

"Is that so. Would you like a cup of tea?" I gestured

for him to sit at the table. "I'll refill the teapot and get you a cup."

"Okay," he said, adding, "Thanks."

Jennifer had finished cleaning up and must have gone to her room. Chef pretended to ignore me, but I could tell he watched my every move.

"I'll fill you in when my guest leaves," I said.

"Why do you believe I am interested?" he asked. "I may be busy when you return."

"I'll take my chances." I poured hot water into the teapot and returned to the table. Parker sat looking at his phone. Young people must miss so much around them with their noses glued to their screens, I thought as I filled his cup and handed it to him.

"Your post said something fell from the plane," he said, getting right to the point.

"Or was pushed out of it."

"Pushed?" he stared at me with his dark eyes. "You know what it was, don't you?"

"No," I answered quickly. Maybe a little too quickly.

Parker's eyes narrowed. "Why are you lying to me?"

His directness took me aback. "I'm not. I think I know what it is, but I have no proof. All the evidence is completely circumstantial."

"That's what they always say."

"Who?"

"People." He seemed to be deciding how much to tell me. "Authorities, mostly. I've reported strange stuff to them before and they always say it's just natural phenomenons or a trick of the light. But I know what I've seen."

I started to wonder if Parker was some sort of conspiracy theorist, so I thought I'd feel him out. "You mean like U.F.O.s?"

He leaned back in the chair, crossing his arms over his chest. "You think I'm some kind of nut."

I was about to say "no" but hoping he'd appreciate some honesty, I said, "I considered the possibility."

He grinned. "You wouldn't be the first to think so. And even though I suspect that U.F.O.s have visited our planet and the government is probably covering it up, I've never seen one myself. What I have seen is drug dealers, smugglers, and even an escaped convict or two. I've been called to testify twice, and my pictures have been used as evidence. And still, the police hardly give me the time of day when I call in a report."

Parker had turned out to be an interesting young man. But should I tell him what I knew or at least suspected?

"It was a body, wasn't it?" he asked.

I was too stunned to respond, but luckily, he didn't wait for me to confirm his theory.

He leaned forward now, excitement in his voice. "See, I knew that plane was up to something because they didn't file a flight plan. Now, you don't have to, but most pilots do unless they're up to something. Then I saw your picture and your caption saying something had been dropped from the plane. At first, I thought for sure it was drugs. Like maybe they planned to take a boat out later and retrieve it or something. But I remembered there was a dead body that washed up on the shore a few days ago by the lighthouse, and boom! I knew that had to be what they dropped from the plane."

"That's what I think too," I said. "My picture was too blurry to read the N-number on the side. But when I put the number from your picture in the FAA database, it came back deregistered with no record of ownership listed."

He pulled a paper out of his pocket and unfolded it on the table between us. "The numbers are painted in red. What if someone took something—maybe red duct tape—and made the numbers look different."

"Like those eights might have been threes?" I asked.

"Exactly. It wouldn't be hard at all."

Leaning over the picture I examined the numbers. "Okay, then let's make a list of all the numbers that this could have been. The eights might have started as threes. Do you think the nine might have been a seven?"

"Possible," he said, writing down different combinations of numbers. He pulled up the FAA website on his phone.

I poured him more tea as he entered each combination into the search bar and waited.

He finally spoke. "Darn." His shoulders slumped in disappointment.

"No luck?" I looked at his picture printout again then pulled up some images of Cessna 172s on my phone. "Check this out." I handed him my phone. "The way the nines are painted, it would be pretty easy to turn a one into an eight, don't you think?"

He grinned and added a few more combinations to the list, then looked those up. "Bingo."

"You got a name?" He showed me his screen. The name, Charles Osman, didn't ring any bells. "I'm calling Deputy Molina right now."

Parker rolled his eyes. "Go ahead, but don't expect him to do much about it."

"I'm sure he will," I said. "This is a murder investigation."

"Maybe so, but I think we should go talk to the guy ourselves," Parker stood, a look of determination on his face.

"Oh, no." I got up and followed him to the door. "At least wait until we hear back from Molina."

He stood staring at his shoes for what felt like a long time before he finally said, "Okay."

"Please tell me you won't go talk to him alone." I felt responsible for this young man. He was barely a man, and I didn't want anything happening to him because of me. "Whoever was in that plane that day might be a murderer."

He puffed up his chest. "I'm not afraid."

"Well, you should be," I snapped. Taking a deep breath, I did my best to soften my voice. "If there's one thing I've learned about murderers, it's that once they've taken a life, they won't hesitate to take another if they feel threatened."

"Look at me," he said, taking a step back and holding his arms out. "I don't make anyone feel threatened. That's the best and the worst part about being me."

"That may be, but the killer will feel threatened the moment they figure out you're onto them." I watched for signs he understood how serious the situation was. "You might not get a warning."

"Uh-huh," he said, his posture still defiant.

I forced my voice to steady, despite my frustration. "With that attitude, you might just end up dead."

CHAPTER 13

*P*arker agreed to wait until we heard back from Deputy Molina. I hoped he meant it. After I called Molina and left a message, I went upstairs to my office to see what I could learn about the pilot.

While it sounded like an uncommon name to me, when I searched for Charles Osman, I got more than nine million results. I narrowed it down, first trying "Charles Osman pilot," which narrowed the results to two million. Next, I tried "Charles Osman Serenity Cove," but that narrowed it down to zero hits.

I combined his name with every town in our small county, and finally got a hit with "Charles Osman Hiverton." A social media post said he was a real estate agent for Hiverton Realty.

Searching through his information, I looked for a connection between him and Eric Vitello. There didn't seem to be one.

In his picture, dated ten years earlier, he didn't look like a murderer. It showed a moderately handsome middle-aged man with beady eyes and heavy dark eyebrows. For all I knew, he was a perfectly nice guy, but if I ran into him in a dark alley, I'd run the other way.

I pulled up the website for Hiverton Realty, but Charles wasn't listed as a current employee. Maybe he'd lost his job and fallen on hard times, working as a hit man on the side to make ends meet.

If someone hired Charles to get rid of Sandra's husband, then who?

The obvious choice, of course, was Sandra. Her alibi wouldn't mean much if she paid someone to do her dirty work. I leaned back in my chair and stared out the window at the ocean. Why would Sandra kill her husband? Money was a powerful motive, of course, but she might have done well financially in a divorce. California was a community property state, after all.

Unless she had a prenuptial agreement.

Facing the computer screen again, I looked to see if there would be any information about a prenup. Not surprisingly, the information wasn't available on public sources. Molina probably knew. He'd also know if Eric Vitello had a hefty insurance policy.

The chance of Molina sharing any of that information with me was slim. But if I didn't ask, the chance would be exactly zero. I called his number again, but when it went to voice mail, I didn't leave another message. In the morning, I'd call and demand some answers.

THE NEXT MORNING, my resolve to demand answers from Molina began to weaken. I decided to start by asking nicely and see how that went. If I met with him in person, perhaps I could convince him, especially if I brought him a box of freshly baked muffins.

Jennifer raised her eyebrows when I told her I'd be back after a quick stop at the police station.

She gestured to the bag of muffins. "If those don't get him talking, I don't know what can. They're dope."

"Dope?" I asked. "I didn't put anything in them. Though, if he doesn't tell me what I want to know…"

Jennifer snorted a laugh. "Don't. Just don't."

"Okay, I won't." I waited for a response, but she was still laughing. "Well, see ya."

During the short drive to the police station, I called Freddie. "What does dope mean?"

"Do we need to have a talk?" she asked.

"Like if someone says my muffins are dope," I clarified.

"Oh, that means really good. It sounds like you're in your car. Where are you headed on a Saturday morning?"

For a moment, I considered telling her I was running an errand, but I knew she'd see right through me. Somehow, she could always tell when I was keeping something from her. "I'm on my way to see Deputy Molina. He hasn't been returning my calls. I'm guessing he'll be working even though it's Saturday since he's in the middle of a murder investigation."

"Have you ever considered the police might be able

to handle the investigation without your help?" she asked.

"No, not really," I said, only partly kidding. "Besides, as a concerned citizen who witnessed a crime and found a dead body, I think it's reasonable to expect to be kept in the loop."

"I see," Freddie said, though I could hear the doubt in her voice. "Let me know if Deputy Molina agrees with you."

"Is there any information about Eric Vitello's cause of death that you're willing to share with me?"

Instead of answering my question, she asked, "Are you busy tonight? I could stop by, especially if you had a shepherd's pie left over from lunch."

I grinned, hoping that meant she was willing to share information. "I'll set aside some for you."

Just as I ended the call, I pulled into the city hall parking lot. I knew the way to Molina's office, so I slipped past the information desk before the woman behind it noticed me.

No one sat at the front desk in the area that served as the police station, but I knew my way to Molina's office. Giving the door a quick tap, I pushed it open and stepped inside. Deputy Molina looked up from his desk and frowned.

"Good morning, Deputy Molina," I said. "I brought you home-baked muffins. Do you have a minute?" I set the bag of muffins on his desk.

"No," he answered quickly, eyeing the bag hungrily. "I am in the middle of a murder investigation, in case you forgot."

I sat down across from him. "Did you question the pilot of the plane?"

He seemed to be deciding whether to answer my question or kick me out of his office. He sighed. "The person you identified was not up in his plane on the day in question."

"Well, of course he's going to say that."

Molina leaned forward, his elbows on the desk. "He has a witness. He was on firm ground at the time you took the picture of the plane. You got the numbers wrong."

That didn't seem possible. "I'd agree with you if the numbers had come back as a plane belonging to someone in Duluth or Philadelphia. But he lives right here in our county. The odds seem astronomical."

"Be that as it may, we spoke to the gentleman who was with him, and his story checks out. Now, if you don't mind, I have work to do."

"Fine," I said. "We'll talk more later." What a waste of my delicious muffins. I hurried out of the office before he could disagree.

When I returned home, I sent Parker a message telling him our clue hadn't panned out, and that the pilot we'd identified wasn't flying the plane I saw. I ended my message with: *Thanks for trying to help.*

I CALLED my brother on his cell phone to check in, still hoping that he, Lulu, and I could spend some time together.

"Lulu and I are going for a drive up the coast," he said. "Would you like to join us? I thought we'd stop for lunch at Cape Mendocino or Eureka. Maybe do some wine tasting on the way back."

My shoulders tensed. "I have a tearoom to run. The weekends are our busiest time."

"Fine," he said. "No need to get in a huff about it."

"Sorry," I said automatically, not sure why I was apologizing. "If you get back in time, why don't the two of you come for dinner?" Had he purposely chosen to invite me when he knew I wouldn't be able to join them?

"We'll see," he said, but I knew better than to expect him to follow through.

The tearoom filled up shortly after we opened and stayed full the entire day. We nearly sold out of shepherd's pie, Saturday's lunch special, but I managed to set one aside for Freddie.

"It hasn't been this busy since summer," Jennifer said as she carried dishes to the sink. "I'm beat."

"Your feet must be killing you. You should run upstairs and put your slippers on."

She grinned. "That's a great idea," she said, then ran up the stairs as if she had all the energy in the world. Oh, to be young again.

Freddie arrived with a bottle of chilled white wine, and I motioned to the table by the front window where I had everything set up.

"Do you need a corkscrew?" I asked.

"It has a twist-off top. I used to be such a snob

about it, but it's so convenient. And some really good wines use twist-offs."

"Your shepherd's pie will be ready in a few minutes," I said, taking a seat.

Freddie sat across from me and poured us each a glass of wine. I let her take a few sips before I asked her what I was itching to find out.

"So..." I began. "Have you finished the autopsy?"

"The sheriff's office put a lot of pressure on me to finish my examination quickly. The funeral is planned for Monday, and I understand the family wants to see the body go in the ground."

"That seems odd," I said.

"Not really." Freddie leaned back in her chair. She looked exhausted. "Everyone grieves differently, and everyone handles funerals their own way, either because of their religion or family traditions. A lot of people need the closure of seeing the casket lowered into the ground. It helps them accept that their loved one is really gone." Her faraway look made me wonder if she had her father in mind. It hadn't been that long since he passed away.

She hadn't told me what I wanted to know, but I tried my best to be patient.

"I'll check on your dinner." When I entered the kitchen, the aroma of gravy and spices filled my nose. I pulled the casserole from the oven, placed it on a plate, and returned to Freddie. Setting it in front of her, I warned her it was hot.

Freddie chuckled. "The bubbling gravy and steaming potatoes should have been my first hint. It smells delicious, but I'm going to wait a few minutes before I take a bite."

"That's wise," I said. "Um, so about the autopsy."

Freddie got my hint. "Cause of death was drowning."

"Drowning?" I asked, not sure I'd heard right. "So, he was still alive when he entered the water?"

"Yes. But he may have been unconscious. He had a blow to the back of the head which caused significant injury. However, he had salt water in his lungs. That and other substantiating factors led me to conclude that he drowned."

"Do you think they hit him over the head before they threw him out of the plane?" I asked.

"No," she said. "I don't."

"Huh? You think he was conscious when he fell?"

"No." She leaned forward and said, "That man did not fall from a plane."

"What?" Now I was really confused. "But it must have been. It's too much of a coincidence that I saw something that looked like a body dropped into the ocean on Sunday and then a body washes ashore on Wednesday."

"April, even a fall of twenty feet would likely have resulted in some sort of injuries. I did a thorough examination of the victim, and the only injury I found was the head injury. That is simply not consistent with a fall from a plane unless it was flying just above the water, practically skimming the waves."

"It wasn't." I tried to estimate how high the plane had been. "It was pretty low, I thought at the time, but it had to be at least fifty feet. Probably higher than that."

Taking a sip of my wine, I tried to make sense of what I'd just been told, but I couldn't. Could it really be just a coincidence that something the same size and shape as a body fell from a plane around the same time that a man fell into the ocean and drowned?

"Then what fell from the plane?" I asked.

Freddie shrugged. "We may never know." She paused, and I could tell she wanted to say more.

Instead of pushing her, I suggested her dinner might be cool enough to eat.

She put a forkful in her mouth and closed her eyes. "Delicious."

As hard as it was, I stayed quiet while she ate.

She'd finished about half her dish when she stopped and put her fork down. "I may get in trouble for telling you, but there's something you really need to know."

"What's that?" I asked, taking a sip of my wine and hoping for a juicy clue.

"Molina got a search warrant for the Vitello home. He didn't find anything suspicious and no evidence of an altercation or foul play. But what he did find were fingerprints belonging to a known felon."

It took me a moment to speak. "There's an ex-con in town? What do we know about him?"

"First," she began, "Vitello's home is in a different town. Second, the fingerprints belong to a woman. Her name is Jamie Jackson. We don't have any reason to think she's still in town, but it's a possibility."

That was unexpected. "What was this woman convicted of?"

"Manslaughter. She killed her boyfriend, who was also a criminal—they'd both been convicted of petty crimes before. Sounds like they were a couple of grifters."

"Why only manslaughter?"

"The D.A. didn't think he could get a murder charge to stick since she claimed self defense, so they worked out a plea bargain. She got out of prison two years ago."

I leaned back in my chair. "Interesting."

"I'm only telling you, so you'll know how serious this is. You need to stay out of trouble." She waited for a reply, but when I hesitated, she added, "Are you listening to me?"

"What? Oh yes, of course." My mind furiously worked to fit this new piece into the puzzle. "Is there any connection between this woman and Sandra or Eric?"

"None that I know of. There's any number of reasons why she might have been inside their home. Molina's checked out their cleaning service, but there are other legitimate possibilities. Or, she might have broken in planning to rob them and got scared off before she took anything."

"Oh! Maybe she was hired to get rid of Eric."

Freddie closed her eyes tightly, took a deep breath in, and let it out slowly. "Did you hear what I said? This woman is dangerous."

"So, you're saying she might be a hit-woman," I suggested.

Freddie picked up her fork and waved it at me. "I'm saying that you need to stay out of it."

"Right," I said, my mind humming with new possibilities.

Exasperated, she banged the fork on the table three times before demanding, "I want you to promise me, April May."

"Oh, sure," I said, my fingers crossed on my lap. "Don't let your dinner get cold."

CHAPTER 14

Sunday turned out to be another unusually busy day considering it was off season, and I wondered why. I complained to Jennifer that it made it difficult to plan when I didn't know how many people would show up for lunch or afternoon tea.

"The weather has been gorgeous these past several days," she said. "And way hotter inland. Maybe more people are up for a drive to the beach. If you end up in Serenity Cove, there's not much else to do besides lying on the beach or coming here. The Mermaid Cafe doesn't even open until four."

"I wonder if that's it. I'm going to start tracking the weather and see if there's a correlation between warmer weather and our sales. Our freezer is almost empty even with all the cooking I've been doing lately."

Jennifer wiped her hands on a dishtowel and pulled her phone out of her apron pocket. "We'll be able to test the theory soon. It's supposed to cool way down in the next few weeks. Highs in the fifties."

I pretended to shiver and rubbed my arms. "Time to break out the winter clothes. Oh! It will be perfect weather to make gumbo. I've been wanting to make it for months, but you have to stand over a hot oven stirring the roux for nearly an hour."

"Mmm..." Jennifer rubbed her belly. "I can't wait to try it."

I didn't tell her I'd wanted to make it ever since I found out that Chef Emile was raised in Louisiana. With his help, I had a feeling my gumbo would be a huge hit.

After our last guests of the day left, I watched Jennifer fill the dishwasher and start it running. What would she think if she knew a ghost stood a few feet away from her, leaning against the counter sipping on a glass of red wine?

Just as I decided I should tell Jennifer that the ghost of Chef Emile Toussaint haunted my kitchen, the sound of the front door opening and closing distracted me.

"I need to remember to lock the front door when the last guest leaves," I said as I pulled my apron off, intending to greet whoever had arrived.

Parker burst through the kitchen door. "I got the name of the witness," he told me. No sooner were the words out of his mouth when he realized we weren't alone. His face reddened and he smiled shyly at Jennifer. "Hello."

"Hi," Jennifer said, adding with characteristic directness, "Who are you?"

"I'm Parker," he said. "I'm helping your mom with an investigation."

Jennifer grinned. "She's *like* a mom, but she's not actually my mom." His words seemed to sink in, and she cocked her head. "What investigation?"

"I'm helping her figure out who was flying the plane that dumped something in the ocean." His confidence seemed to return as he spoke. "Small planes are a special interest of mine."

"Oh, really?" Jennifer smiled. "Mine is antiques and period costumes." She looked from Parker to me. "Well, see you later."

"Nice meeting you too, um..." Parker began. "What's your name?"

"Jennifer. Well, see you around."

Parker watched her take the back staircase two steps at a time before returning his attention to me. "So, after your last message I went to see the pilot—"

"What? I thought we agreed you wouldn't go talk to him alone."

He shrugged. "You agreed. But I figured if he wasn't a murderer then it would be safe to talk to him." He smiled tentatively. "I got the name of the guy he says he was with at the time. If we can poke holes in his story..."

I shook my head. "The coroner told me that the dead man didn't fall from a plane. He would have sustained injuries, which he didn't. It was just your basic drowning. I heard that he was a heavy drinker, so maybe he got drunk and fell overboard."

"Oh." Parker seemed disappointed. "Still..." He

frowned, staring at one of the cupboards as if trying to figure something out.

"It's quite a coincidence," I said.

He scratched his jaw as he thought this over. "A coincidence? Something body-shaped fell from a plane around the same time that someone drowned. And in the same general area. You call that a coincidence?"

I struggled to make sense of everything, but I couldn't. Another thing nagged at my mind. "And I just happened to get a text right at that time telling me the dolphins were running."

"That's too much of a coincidence if you ask me," he said. "I'm going to do some more digging. Maybe I can turn up something about Charles Osman."

Parker had me wondering if the pilot was innocent as he claimed. "Just don't go talking to him alone again, please? If anything happens to you—"

He shrugged. "Don't worry. I'll do all my digging online, I promise."

CHAPTER 15

*M*onday morning, the day of Sandra's husband's funeral, I slipped into a navy-blue dress I'd bought for a work event a couple of years earlier, happy to be able to wear it a second time. Maybe happy wasn't the right word considering the occasion. It would be an outdoor service, so I wore flats in case I had to walk across grassy areas. There were few things more annoying than trying to walk with high heels sinking into the ground.

When I arrived at Irma's and got out of the car, she stepped out of her front door. She wore a long black dress along with a small hat with a veil covering her face. I did my best not to snicker. It seemed a bit over-done considering she'd never met the deceased.

"Nice hat," I said as I opened the passenger door for her.

"It's called a fascinator," she informed me. "I bought it back in 1967 and I've worn it at every funeral I've attended."

"Who died in '67?" I wanted to know who had meant enough to her to make the purchase.

"Ah, heck. I don't remember," she said. "That was a long time ago. I saw this hat in the window at I. Magnin's on a visit to San Francisco. My mama insisted that I go to a funeral with her for some relative we hardly ever saw. Anyway, I told her the only way I'd go was if she bought me this hat."

"And she did."

"Obviously." Once Irma had settled herself in the car and buckled her seat belt, she asked, "Why are we going to this funeral, anyway? And don't say to pay our respects. I can see right through you."

"We're going to support Sandra and Cheryl," I explained.

"Oh, right. Your new hoity-toity friends. I hope you're not planning to dump me as soon as they finish their enrollment process. If they make you go streaking through the town in your panties and bra, give me a call, okay?"

"I'm not pledging a sorority, Irma." I chuckled in spite of myself. "I just wanted to have friends to do things with, like painting class and going to brunch." Friends my own age, I added silently.

"I'll go to brunch with you anytime," she said. "Although it's not as much fun when I have to watch what I eat." She frowned. "You got me thinking of eggs Benedict again, and now I'm hungry."

"I've got a granola bar in my purse you're welcome to have."

Irma slunk down in her seat and pouted. She was

barely five feet tall, and I wondered if she could see out the window from that position. We drove in silence most of the way to the funeral home in Somerton. She seemed to perk up as we got closer.

She grinned. "It just occurred to me that a funeral might be a great place to meet men." She pulled a lipstick out of her purse and flipped down the visor to use the mirror. "Let me know if you think you're going to hit a bump."

We turned down the road to the funeral home, and I followed a line of cars into the parking lot.

"I thought we were early," I said, surprised by the traffic. "I hope we can find a space."

"Wow." Irma took in all the limousines and luxury cars ahead and behind us. "I didn't know the dead guy was famous. No one has this many friends."

At a loss to explain the crowd, I concentrated on parking in the last available spot. The SUV in front of us had considered it before passing by, probably because their massive vehicle wouldn't fit.

Irma and I got out of the car and followed the mourners to a field set up with folding chairs. I would have thought we were attending a wedding except for the location. Besides, there were way more flowers than I'd ever seen in one place.

We found seats in the last row and waited. Irma's eyes roamed the crowd, probably looking for her next boyfriend. She must have been pleased by the number of affluent-looking older men in attendance.

When the service began, we quickly understood the reason for the large turnout. Eric Vitello had not only been the vice president of a tech firm, but he also sat on the board of several non-profits and made large donations to a number of others.

I craned my neck attempting to see if Sandra sat up front. I spotted her blonde hair. She hung her head low as if praying and dabbed at her eyes with a lace handkerchief. Cheryl sat on her right with Debbie on the left. After scanning the crowd seated in front of us, I looked off to the sides where groups of latecomers stood listening to the eulogies.

Standing by a tree apart from the others, Sheriff Fontana wore a dark suit. Of course, he would be here. He was Cheryl's husband and Cheryl was one of Sandra's closest friends, but why wasn't he with his wife?

He made eye contact and nodded. I nodded back and returned to listening to the speakers.

Irma leaned closer and whispered. "How long is this going to last? I'm going to need to pee if it goes on much longer."

Her comment nearly made me break out in laughter, and I struggled to keep my composure. "If you need to go, just go. I'm sure there are restrooms around here somewhere." Cheryl stood and stepped away from the chairs. I pointed. "That's probably where Cheryl's going. Just keep an eye on her."

Cheryl didn't look happy, but I had trouble deciphering her expression from so far away. Was she angry? As she walked, she began talking to a man who fell in step with her. Or was he talking to her?

She stared straight ahead as if ignoring him while

he continued to talk. The man glanced over his shoulder and my heart nearly skipped a beat. His beady eyes and thick eyebrows were unmistakable. It was the pilot.

By the time I nudged Irma, the pilot had walked off in the opposite direction.

"What?" she asked in a loud whisper.

"That man," I began, but didn't know what else to say. I hadn't told her any of the details about the pilot. "I'll explain later."

She crossed her arms over her chest. "I'm bored. What a waste of a perfectly good morning."

"We'll leave in a minute." I wanted time to think. I needed to know how all the pieces fit together. Now I was sure that Charles Osman had dropped something from his plane. Something that was meant to look like a body.

And I was meant to see the plane and whatever fell from it that day. That's why I got the text.

But why?

To give "the girls" alibis? Did they not realize that the coroner would be able to tell that the body had not been dropped from the plane?

Pulling a pen from my purse, I dug around for something to write on, settling on a parking stub. I wrote a note.

The funeral seemed to be wrapping up, and we were all being invited to the gravesite and then to a reception.

I nudged Irma. "Let's go."

We rose along with everyone else, and I led Irma to

where the sheriff stood. A number of people had also made their way over to him. Apparently, being the sheriff made one popular.

I tucked the note in my palm, hoping to pass it to him without anyone else noticing. "Sheriff Fontana." I shook his hand and passed him the note. His eyebrows rose as he slipped the note into his pocket.

As soon as we were in the car, I began filling Irma in on Cheryl and Charles Osman, the pilot.

"Cheryl must be in on it somehow," I said. "It's some sort of coverup."

"How?" she asked as I pulled into her driveway. "And why?"

My phone buzzed, and I glanced at the screen.

"It's my brother," I said as she opened the car door. "Asking where I am. As if I haven't been trying to get together with him for days. It's all about him. He never even considers the fact that I have responsibilities."

Irma stopped with one foot out the door and turned back with a sympathetic look. "Family can really get on your nerves, can't they?"

I laughed. "Thanks for letting me rant. I feel better now."

"Anytime," Irma said and climbed out of the car. "Call me if you sense a sequel to your rant after you spend some time with them."

"You're a good friend," I said, but she merely grunted a response and slammed the car door shut.

After sending Jeff a message offering to take him and Lulu to lunch, the drive to the hotel took only a few minutes. I loved being able to get almost anywhere in town in five minutes or less. The downside was there weren't many places to go in town. We didn't have a movie theater or shopping mall, but it was a tradeoff I was happy to make.

I parked and entered the boutique hotel, expecting Jeff to be waiting. After a few minutes, I sent another message and took a seat in the lobby to wait. I hadn't talked to Jeff since Lulu had told me they'd come to town to claim their inheritance. I wondered if he'd bring it up during lunch.

The elevator doors chimed as they opened and Jeff and Lulu stepped out. They both appeared sullen for some reason, but Lulu pasted on a big smile the moment she saw me.

She hurried over to hug me. "I'm so glad I got to see you before we left."

"Left?" Would they really leave after spending so little time with me?

Jeff cleared his throat. "Lulu told me what you said to her. I don't appreciate you spreading your lies to my wife."

"What are you talking about?" I asked. "What lies?"

Jeff scowled. "It's bad enough you've stolen my inheritance, but to try to turn my wife against me— that's beyond anything you've done to me in the past."

I felt my blood begin to boil. "I did not steal your inheritance. Mom had nothing her whole life. You know that. She had nothing when she died and that's what she left us. Nothing."

"That house had to be worth a half-mill in today's market."

"That was my house." I couldn't figure out why he was being so stubborn. "I asked you if you wanted to help buy a place for Mom to live but you said no. So, I did. You know this. Why are you pretending otherwise?"

Jeff jutted his chin forward and took a step closer to me. I resisted the impulse to retreat. If he thought he could intimidate me into giving in, he would find out how wrong he was.

"I'll be calling my lawyer in the morning," he said. "Forget about lunch. And forget about ever seeing us again." He grabbed Lulu's elbow and guided her away. I felt glued to the spot as they stepped into the elevator, and I watched the doors close.

The desk clerk stepped out from behind the counter. She came over to me and spoke gently. "Ms. May? Is everything all right?"

"No, it's not," I said, then mustered something of a smile. "Just family stuff."

She nodded in agreement. "Families can be complicated."

"No kidding," I said. "By the way, you have my credit card on file for Jeffrey May. I'll pay the room for tonight, but I'm not authorizing him and his wife to charge anything else."

"Got it," she said. "I'll make a note of that. And sorry you and your brother aren't getting along. Sometimes there's only so much you can do. I'm sure he'll come around eventually."

I wasn't so sure.

CHAPTER 16

*N*o sooner had I unlocked my back door and stepped into the kitchen when my phone buzzed again. I greeted Chef, who slowly stirred a pot on the stove, but he didn't look up or acknowledge my presence. Was he mad at me?

"Everything okay?" I asked, but he ignored my question.

Pulling my phone from my purse, I saw a text from an unknown number. *Can you meet me at Bub's Bar & Grill at 6PM?* The last time I'd been to Bub's, a dive bar in Hiverton, was when Molina asked me to meet him there, but something told me this text wasn't from Molina.

Who is this? I texted back, staring at the phone for several long seconds waiting for the reply.

Good job palming the note," came the answer.

I wrote *Sheriff Fontana?* but realized just before I hit send that he might not want our messages to be tracked back to him. I hit backspace and typed *I'll be there.*

A quick glance at the clock told me I had thirty minutes before I had to leave, so I made myself a sandwich. Bub's might call itself a Bar and Grill, but I had no interest in trying out their food. It was also the opposite of fancy, so I threw on jeans, a T-shirt, and a zippered sweatshirt.

On the drive, I thought about what to say to the sheriff. "I'll just tell him the truth," I told myself. "Just the facts." I'd made my own conclusions. There were already too many coincidences regarding Vitello's death, and I didn't believe that Charles Osman speaking to Cheryl at the funeral was just a random interaction. Had she paid the pilot to drop a body-shaped object from his plane and then lie about it? Was the pilot asking her for more money to keep his secret?

Everyone knew that helping cover up a murder was dangerous enough without trying to extort those involved. I struggled to understand why the sheriff's wife, a pillar of the community, would get involved in murdering one of her friends' husbands.

My mind whirred with the possibilities. Had Sandra's husband been a horrible man and the women decided they needed to take care of him?

That didn't make any sense. Wouldn't she have gone to her husband first since he was the county sheriff. Or... maybe she had. Maybe they had no proof of what Sandra's husband had done.

I struggled to reconcile that Eric Vitello—a man who'd been portrayed at the funeral as a caring, compassionate person who everyone seemed to admire —might have been cruel to his wife.

If Cheryl was involved in the murder in some way, was I putting myself in danger by talking to the sheriff? I shook off the thought. I'd never known anyone who was more of a rule follower and couldn't imagine him getting involved in a murder plot. I'd have to trust my gut which told me to trust him.

The sun dipped below the buildings as I drove through the dreary town. I turned down a deserted looking street and pulled up in front of Bub's, one of only a few cars parked there. Monday probably wasn't their big night.

After a few deep breaths to steel myself for whatever I was getting myself into, I stepped out of the car and pushed open the door, stepping inside the dimly lit bar. My eyes quickly adjusted to the lack of light, and I scanned the room.

Fontana looked up as I reached his table and slid into the vinyl-upholstered booth. Two mugs of beer sat in front of him, and he pushed one of them across to me.

"You don't have to drink it if you don't want to," he said.

Assuming he didn't want us to stick out like two sore thumbs, I took a sip. "I like a beer now and then." When he raised an eyebrow, I added, "Did you think I survived on nothing but tea?'

"I suppose I did." He took a long gulp from his mug and then looked me in the eye. "You're probably wondering why I chose this charming establishment for our meeting."

"No," I said jokingly. "Seems the perfect place for the county sheriff to invite a tearoom operator out for a beer."

"You know the man who talked to my wife at the funeral, don't you?"

I nodded but got distracted by a man sitting at the bar. He appeared to be looking at his phone, but now and then he would hold it up and point it in our direction. "Listen carefully," I said. "I'm going to tell you something, and you're going to want to turn around and look. But don't. Okay?"

He leaned forward, put his elbows on the table, and whispered, "Someone's watching us, aren't they?"

"They sure are. And it looks like they're taking pictures."

"Follow my lead," Fontana said, his voice low. "Wait a minute or so and then leave. I'll be in touch." More loudly, he said, "Well, I gotta run. Good seeing you again."

As soon as Fontana stood and headed for the back door, the stranger put his phone away and held his head down. While he was distracted, I took the opportunity to take a picture of him.

Once I was back in my car, I realized I hadn't learned anything except that someone was following either me or Fontana. It must have been Fontana he was after, since I couldn't think of any reason why someone would be watching me. Besides, the stranger was already there when I arrived, so he must have followed the sheriff there.

I'd trusted my gut when it told me I could trust the sheriff. Now my gut was telling me to get the heck out of there.

~

THE NEXT MORNING, I awoke to a text from Parker wanting to know if I had any updates on the "case." He seemed like a nice kid, but I regretted getting him involved. He didn't seem to realize how dangerous it was to poke your nose in where a killer didn't want it.

Jennifer had spent the night at her grandmother's. She hadn't moved any of her things yet, but I already missed seeing her smiling face in the morning. I considered turning on the espresso machine but didn't want to bother just for one cup of cappuccino. Also, machinery and I didn't always get along, and I was a little afraid of blowing up the kitchen.

I could make a pot of coffee. Or a pot of tea. Maybe English Breakfast tea with a splash of milk the way they drank it in the U.K. Luckily, while I was stuck in indecision, Irma arrived.

She stomped her walking stick on the tile floor. "Aren't we walking today?"

"Oh," I said. "What day is it?"

"It's Tuesday." She took a seat at the island. "I don't see Jennifer, so I guess that means I don't get a non-fat decaf latte today."

"I'll put a pot on, and I can bring you up to date on

119

what's happened." I filled the carafe with water. "Unless you're really set on going for a walk."

"I can skip a day, I suppose."

While the coffee brewed, I found a couple of carrot muffins in the freezer, wrapped them in foil, and put them in the oven at 350 degrees. The microwave wasn't made for baked goods, in my opinion.

Once the coffee had finished brewing, I filled two cups. I handed Irma one and began to tell her about my meeting with Sheriff Fontana.

"Why is he being all secretive?" she asked.

"I think Cheryl, his wife, might be involved somehow with the murder." Before she could interrupt me, I held up a hand. "I don't know what or why, but that guy at the funeral? He's the pilot I told you about. He's got something to do with the murder, and she knows him, so…"

"Seems a pretty sketchy connection," Irma said. "Lots of somehows and somethings. Did you ever think it might just be, I don't know…?"

"A coincidence?" I sighed. "There are way, way too many coincidences involving one dead body. I'm pretty sure that it's statistically impossible."

"Since when are you an expert on statistics?"

I shrugged. "I'm just saying it seems highly unlikely."

"And I think it's highly unlikely that a society lady married to the county sheriff was involved in a murder."

She had a point. "What about a cover up?"

"Hmmm…" She drummed her fingers on the side of her cup. "That sounds more plausible. You're saying that someone killed Sandra's husband and Cheryl helped cover it up?"

"Right. They—whoever was the mastermind—figured that dropping the body from the plane would make everyone think that Eric Vitello was killed Sunday morning. But what if he wasn't?"

"That would mean a lot of people don't have alibis," Irma said, getting the picture.

"Or one person in particular. Sandra."

"They do say it's almost always the spouse," Irma said. "But why would she kill her husband? And a bigger question is why Cheryl would help her cover it up?"

"An excellent question." One I didn't have the answer for.

Irma claimed she had things to do, which wasn't surprising considering she ran a restaurant that was open seven days a week. Since I'd decided to stay open only four days a week, local residents had been pressuring Irma to open the Mermaid Cafe for lunch. Someone even started a petition, but they didn't know Irma the way I did. She'd sooner close down the restaurant altogether rather than let anyone else tell her how to run it.

I usually put together my shopping list on Mondays, so I had plenty of time to replenish supplies, bake, and cook. With the funeral and my meeting with Sheriff Fontana, I never got around to it until now. As I checked the refrigerator's crisper drawers to see what had gone bad and needed replacing, I thought I heard a knock on the door. Glancing at the clock I saw it was noon. I thought everyone knew we weren't open on Tuesdays anymore. The knock repeated, harder this time.

When I opened the front door, Parker stood on the front porch gazing out at the ocean.

"Hey, Parker," I said.

He glanced over his shoulder at me then turned back to face the water. "How do you get anything done around here? I'd just stare at the waves all day."

I knew just what he meant. "I did that a lot when I first moved in. It's incredibly relaxing."

"Almost hypnotic," he said, his voice in a daze. He shook off his stupor and grinned. "Well, you told me not to do any snooping on my own, so here I am."

"Huh?" I took a seat in one of the wooden chairs on the porch.

Parker followed my lead and sat down across from me. "There's a commuter airport about ten miles from here, and I'm thinking that's where the plane must have taken off from. I called and talked to this guy I know who runs the flight school there. He lets me hang out in his office sometimes. It has an awesome view of the apron." He must have picked up on my confusion, because he added, "You know, the runways and where the planes park and stuff. Lots of people call it the tarmac, but that's not actually the right word for it."

"I see."

"Sorry—I kind of geek out about planes and airports. Watching the planes take off and land is a lot like watching the ocean waves for me. It helps me chill out. I'm going to get my pilot's license as soon as I save enough money."

"Let's get back to the snooping part," I said, waiting for him to explain.

"He said I could come by this afternoon. I figured maybe we could find out about that plane."

"But we know the body wasn't dropped from a plane. The plane has nothing to do with the murder."

"You sure about that?" he asked.

I didn't know how to answer him, especially after seeing Cheryl talking to the pilot. There were too many coincidences, and they just didn't add up.

"Why would someone drop something from a plane, and what does it have to do with the murder?" I asked, asking myself as much as him.

"It was meant to look like a body," Parker said, his voice becoming more animated.

I nodded. "And I was meant to see it. I got a text telling me the dolphins were running shortly before I saw the plane. I assumed the text was from Bree, because she's really into dolphins. She's friends with Sandra and Cheryl."

"What's the number?" Parker asked.

I pulled out my phone and showed him the text. He took it from me and hit dial, but the number rang and rang. No answer and no voice mail.

"Probably a burner phone." Parker stood. "So, what are we waiting for?"

CHAPTER 17

*T*he airport might have been ten miles away as the crow flies, but it took more than a half hour to get there on local roads that wove around the hilly landscape. As we got closer, the land became flat and we passed industrial buildings, a junkyard, and a microbrewery. I hoped the pilots waited until after their flights before stopping in for a beer.

The street ended at the airport. I pulled into the parking lot next to a corrugated building with a low roof. A rusty-looking sign on the side said, "Learn to Fly Here."

Parker and I entered the building through a pair of heavy doors and found ourselves in a large room. To the right, a folding table held a carafe of coffee and paper cups.

"Flying lessons here include all the coffee you can drink for a quarter a cup. It's on the honor system." Parker gestured to a coffee can with a slit in the plastic top. "Want a cup?"

Coffee sounded good, but when I saw the powdered creamer, I decided against it. I followed Parker down a narrow hall. I waited outside a small office while Parker went in, greeting the silver-haired man who sat behind a small, metal desk.

"Hey, Parker. I didn't know you were bringing someone with you." Before Parker could respond, the man stood and waved at me to enter. He wore jeans and a short-sleeved button-collared shirt and a huge smile. "I'm Earl Donovan." He reached out his hand. "We don't get many lovely ladies like yourself around here."

"I'm April May." I took his hand. He held onto mine longer than was necessary but not long enough to be creepy. "Nice to meet you, Earl."

"Have a seat." Earl hurried to grab me a folding chair which he set in front of his desk. "There's one for you over there," he told Parker, who retrieved another chair from the corner of the room.

"You thinking of learning to fly, April?" Earl asked once he'd returned to his seat behind the desk.

"I don't think so. I'm looking for a new hobby, but I prefer to let someone else fly the plane when I travel."

"Well, if you change your mind, you let me know. I'll give you a special rate for private lessons." He said this with a friendly wink.

"Thanks," I said. "That's very kind of you."

Parker wore a puzzled look, possibly not understanding why someone would be making such a fuss over a middle-aged woman like me.

After offering us coffee, Earl got right to the point.

"So, if you're not here for flying lessons, what did you want to see me about?"

I sat back and listened while Parker explained about the plane that had flown over Serenity Cove a week and a half earlier. "The pilot claims he didn't take the plane up that day, but April saw it fly over the ocean by her house. So, if he didn't take it up then somebody else did. The N-number was altered—I think with duct tape. I thought you might be able to tell us if he was lying or not."

"Why all this interest in this plane?" Earl asked.

Parker glanced at me before answering. "It has to do with a murder."

Earl busted out laughing, but as he observed our unsmiling faces, his expression went from amused to doubtful. "You're serious?"

I stepped in. "The plane wasn't involved directly in the murder, but possibly in covering it up." I didn't want to get into any more details, but Parker didn't hesitate to fill him in.

"The pilot dropped something from the plane," he told Earl. "It was the size and shape of a body." He held his arms out to demonstrate. "They must have wanted anyone who saw it to think it was a body. But it was a decoy."

"A decoy?" Earl asked. "Why would anyone want you to think they'd dropped a body from a plane?"

"That's a good question," I said before Parker could answer. "It was meant to throw the police off the track." I didn't want to share all of our theories with

Earl. They were only theories, after all. "The murder happened at right around the same time."

"Ah, yes." Earl's eyes widened as he put two and two together. "That body that was washed up on the shore in Serenity Cove. Wait—where did you say you live?" he asked me.

"I run a tearoom from my house in Serenity Cove, probably a mile and a half from where the body was found." I left out the part about how I had also found the body.

Earl slowly nodded as he figured out what to do with the information we'd given him. "You think the plane and the murder might be connected." He looked from me to Parker and back to me. "You said the N-numbers were doctored, but you figured out who it belonged to, I'm guessing."

"We figured it out together," Parker said. "We make a good team."

I suppressed a laugh and hoped that my young friend wouldn't start coming to me to help him with his conspiracy theories.

"And the plane belongs to...?" Earl prompted.

"Charles Osman." I let the name hang in the air while I waited to see Earl's reaction. He barely moved, but one eye twitched ever so slightly. Parker followed my lead and stayed quiet, waiting to see what Earl would say.

Earl pursed his lips and stared past me. I followed his gaze. On the other side of the window, a plane sped by on the runway and lifted into the sky.

"Charles Osman is a skunk," Earl finally said. "But

you didn't hear it from me. Talking about pilots behind their back isn't good for business."

"We certainly don't want to cause you any trouble," I said. "What we really want to know is whether he took his plane out two Sundays ago."

"No way I'd know unless he filed a flight plan. It's not required if he flew VFR."

"Visual flight rules," Parker said in explanation. "That's when conditions and visibility are good, and the pilot doesn't need to use his instruments to navigate."

"That's right," Earl said. "And if he didn't want anyone to know he had his plane out that day, I doubt he filed one."

"Gotcha," I said. "But someone might have seen him. Were you working that day?"

"Don't work weekends," he said.

"Is there a sign-in or some kind of security clearance that would track who came and went?"

"Nope. There's a gate behind us with a code." He pointed out the window behind him where I could see a gate set into the fence. "An owner can park and go straight to his plane if he wants. You might have noticed this isn't a busy airport."

"A code?" I asked. "Then there's an electronic log of who comes and goes using it."

Earl shook his head. "Sorry, my dear. It's not anything hi-tech like that."

"Darn," I said. This trip was turning out to be a waste of time.

"On the other hand, someone might have seen him,"

Earl said. "Around what time are we talking about?"

"I'd say around nine-thirty or ten A.M.," I said.

"Tell you what. I'll ask around and see who was here that day. A week ago, last Sunday, you say?"

"That's right."

"If you'd like to give me your number, April, I'll call you if I learn anything. Maybe we could go out for coffee sometime. Or a drink. Your call."

Parker had enough of Earl flirting with me. "You have my number, Earl." He turned to me. "Let's go."

I gave Earl a smile and thanked him. He handed me his card. "If you change your mind, give me a call."

By the time Tuesday evening rolled around, I could hardly wait to go to painting class, and not just to practice my art skills.

Cheryl and Debbie arrived together just as class began. I wasn't surprised that Sandra didn't join us. Ron, the instructor, began with a short lecture on color theory, then gave us our assignment for the evening—continue working on our color wheels.

Debbie might have groaned.

I'd made good progress on my color wheel the previous session, but I had other things on my mind now. As I dabbed at my painting, I watched Cheryl from the corner of my eye for signs of guilt. The only problem was I didn't know what to look for.

The instructor went from easel to easel commenting on the students' progress and offering suggestions. When Ron reached me, he said, "You seem distracted, April. A lot on your mind?"

A few of the colors had run together and turned into a muddy brown. "Maybe I'm not cut out for painting."

"Nonsense," he said. "All you need is some practice." Before he walked away, he added, "A little focus might help, too."

I took his advice and kept my eyes on my painting for the rest of the class. As I cleaned my brush and palette next to Debbie, I looked for Cheryl, but didn't see her.

"Did Cheryl leave?" I asked.

"She better not, since she's my ride," Debbie said with a grin. "She had to make a phone call so she went to her car." She'd finished packing up, so she said good-night. "See you at book club tomorrow?"

"Book club?" I'd forgotten all about it. "Um, sure. See you there."

CHAPTER 18

The next morning after Irma and I returned from our walk, I invited her to join me for coffee. We found Jennifer and Freddie waiting for us in the kitchen.

Jennifer made espresso drinks for Irma and me while I mixed the batter for lemon-ricotta pancakes.

Irma watched me stirring. "Pancakes? They can't be any good if you're serving them to me."

"I'm using low-fat ricotta cheese and replacing half the flour with whole wheat. I'm also using coconut oil to grease the skillet instead of butter."

Irma propped an elbow on the island and put her chin in her hand. "Gee," she said, her sarcastic tone obvious. "Sounds delicious."

I laughed. "Why don't you withhold judgement until you taste them? I even have pure maple syrup, which is not only high in antioxidants and other nutrients but has fewer calories than sugar or honey."

Irma brightened up at the mention of maple syrup, and Freddie said, "Sounds delicious to me."

"None for me, thanks," Jennifer said. "I need to get to history class."

"Ugh, history," Irma said.

Jennifer huffed, "Some people actually enjoy learning about the past, you know. Me, for instance."

I grinned. "Irma's lived through most of history, so she could teach the class using her first-hand knowledge." I turned to Irma. "Did the dinosaurs go extinct before or after you graduated high school?"

Irma tried to shoot me a glare, but she couldn't keep a straight face. "Jerk," she said, but she was smiling so I didn't take it personally.

"If I need help with my homework," Jennifer said, "I know who to ask."

After Jennifer left, I served Irma and Freddie breakfast and sat down to enjoy a short stack myself. I took a forkful and smiled as the sweet and savory flavors hit my tastebuds.

When Irma swallowed her first bite, she brightened. "These are actually really good."

"Really, really good," Freddie commented, adding to Irma. "I don't know why you doubted April. She's a miracle worker in the kitchen."

I felt my face redden. "I think miracle worker might be overstating it, but I'm glad you're enjoying them. This isn't just for your benefit, Irma. My doctor said my cholesterol is too high and if I don't bring it down, I'll have to go on medication."

"Your doctor?" Irma tilted her head to one side. "Freddie isn't your doctor?"

Freddie quickly jumped in. "Not everyone in town comes to me, you know. April probably has a long-time relationship with her doctor. Besides, it can be awkward for some people when their doctor is a friend."

Irma snorted. "If anyone thinks they can keep something secret by going to another town, they'd be wrong."

A TEXT WOKE me from a dream. I'd been laying on a chaise lounge at the hotel with a mimosa in my hand. And a handsome man had been rubbing suntan lotion on my back. I rubbed my eyes as I tried to remember who the man had been, but the memory floated away like vapor.

Frowning at the screen, I saw a phone number I didn't recognize. It wasn't hard to guess the sender.

Can you meet at 8AM? the message asked.

"How many burner phones do you have, Sheriff?" I said out loud, but I texted back, *What's the password?*

I imagined the three blinking dots were Sheriff Fontana rolling his eyes. Eventually, I saw his reply: *No dive bars this time.*

Satisfied that I wasn't being led into a trap, we arranged to meet. He would drop a pin when he reached the parking lot and then walk along a hiking trail before dropping another pin.

The stealthy arrangements kicked my adrenaline up a notch, and I rushed to get dressed. Leaving Jennifer a note, I hopped into my car and drove to the first location—a dirt lot next to a sign with a map of hiking trails. There wasn't a car in sight, which made me nervous.

"Get over yourself, April," I said. He'd probably parked somewhere else after he sent me the location. Still, I wished I had a weapon of some sort. I opened the trunk, but the only thing remotely weapon-like was my umbrella. It would have to do.

I slammed the trunk closed and the sound reverberated in the quiet morning. Glancing at my phone, I saw he'd sent me the next location. But how was I supposed to get from here to there?

As I headed down a dirt path, I became aware of twittering birds, rustling leaves, and the unsettling sound of critters scurrying through the brush. The sun, still low in the sky, threw long shadows across my path. I hadn't realized there were such lovely hiking trails so close to home.

When I reached a fork in the trail, I gazed at my phone not sure which way to go. I heard a noise and looked up. Sheriff Fontana waved at me from further down the right-hand path.

We hiked for nearly half an hour, him staying far ahead of me until we reached a clearing. In front of me stood several majestic weeping willows. I spotted Fontana just as he slipped under the branches of the farthest one.

I felt like a kid again with a secret hiding place as I hurried after him and ducked through the branches.

Fontana stood by the trunk of the willow with his arms crossed over his chest. A smile played on his lips as if he were enjoying our game of secret agent.

He took a couple of beach towels out of his backpack, which he folded and laid them on the ground. He plopped down on one of them. I did the same and leaned back against the tree as he produced a thermos and poured us each a cup of coffee.

"Cream or sugar?" he asked, holding out little packets. "I'm afraid I forgot to bring stirrers."

"Black is fine," I said, although I almost never drank my coffee that way. "What's going on, Sheriff?"

He stared at his coffee and slowly shook his head. "I wish I knew." He took a deep breath and let it out before continuing. "I suspected my wife of keeping secrets from me before I got your note. I tried to ask her what was going on, but she shut me out." He shrugged. "That's nothing new. She's shut me out of her life for the last several years. But this feels different, and I'm getting worried."

I didn't feel comfortable hearing about his marital issues, but I did want to know what she had to do with Sandra's husband's murder.

"Did you ask her how she knew the pilot?" I asked.

He shook his head. "She blew up when I asked her— accused me of having her watched. Which is ironic, considering I'm pretty sure she hired the guy who was watching me at Bub's. I told her I saw them talking at the funeral, but she claims she doesn't know him. Said he asked her where the men's room was."

"She sure seemed like she knew him. She didn't seem at all happy about him talking to her either."

"Not surprising." He took a swig from his mug and grimaced. "Sorry. You're probably used to better quality coffee than this."

We were completely hidden from outside observers by the long, graceful branches of the tree if anyone did happen to pass by.

"It's like a secret hideaway," I said. "Almost as good as a secret garden. Maybe I'll plant one in my back yard."

"You'll plant a secret garden?" he asked.

"I meant a willow tree. But a secret garden would be lovely too."

We sat in silence for several long moments before Fontana said, "I hate to ask you to do this…"

"Do what?"

He grimaced. "Spy on my wife."

I turned to look in his eyes, which sparkled with unshed tears. "Why? What do you think she's doing?"

"That's just it," he said. "I don't know."

"Oh." How did he expect me to help with so little information? "If she wouldn't tell you what she and the pilot were talking about, she's not going to tell me."

He hung his head. "You're probably right."

"Do you think Cheryl might be mixed up in Sandra's husband's murder?" I asked.

"No!" His eyes widened as if he'd surprised himself by his own emotions. "I hope and pray she's not. She's a good woman, April. She's not perfect, mind you, but I can't believe she'd be involved in a murder."

"What about covering up for someone else?"

"What do you know?" he demanded.

"Hey, I'm on your side, remember?"

"Sorry," he said in a softer voice. "I didn't mean to take it out on you."

"Here's the thing," I explained. "Sandra had a convenient alibi when everyone thought that the murderer tossed her husband's body out of a plane. But now that we know that didn't happen, that alibi is pretty useless."

He nodded. "The coroner can't be sure how long Vitello was dead." He paused. "But you knew that already."

I nodded and waited for him to continue.

"So, you think Sandra killed her husband and my wife tried to help her cover it up?" he asked.

"It makes sense to me. Maybe it was an accident, and Cheryl doesn't want Sandra to have to go through possibly being accused of murder or a long, drawn-out trial. Sandra and Eric might have gotten into a fight while they were out on a boat."

"And Sandra pushed her husband overboard? After hitting him over the head?" he asked. "Accidentally?"

I shrugged. After all, I didn't have everything figured out just yet. "Or in self defense."

The sheriff tapped his fingers against his cup as he thought over my theory. "There were rumors that he hit her."

She'd had what looked like bruises on her cheekbone when I'd last seen her. "That's a possibility."

"Just keep your ears and eyes open and let me know if you hear anything that might shed some light on what Cheryl has gotten herself involved with. Would you do that much for me?"

That didn't seem too much to ask. "Okay, I'll do it." I wanted to know what she was up to anyway, but I didn't tell him that.

"I'll let you leave first the same way you came. I'll wait fifteen or twenty minutes and take the other path. Hopefully, if someone followed one of us, they got bored and left."

The moment I pushed through the draping branches to the meadow outside, I felt like I was being watched. More likely, Fontana had made me paranoid with his talk about us being followed. If Cheryl had hired someone, were they following Fontana or me. Or both? And why?

Still, I couldn't shake the feeling of someone's eyes on me until I got into my car and drove away.

CHAPTER 19

As I maneuvered the curvy mountain road on my way to the main highway, I heard my phone chime. I pulled over and read a text from Cheryl reminding me that their book club met that afternoon at the Somerton library.

Remembering how stylishly Cheryl and her friends had dressed for painting class, I headed home to change. My khaki pants and black sweater would be perfectly acceptable for most people, but Cheryl wasn't most people.

I arrived home in plenty of time to make myself lunch. After putting a couple of frozen mini quiches in the oven, I went upstairs to change. My wardrobe consisted of casual, around the house clothes and my tearoom hostess outfits. I opted for one of the latter, hoping I wouldn't feel completely out of place in a flowered dress.

On the drive to Somerton, I let my mind wander. Now that the Serenity Cove library had reopened, it might be nice to start a book club that met there. How many people would join us? Irma, Freddie, and Jennifer, of course, but who else? I wondered if the librarian would be able to join us. Maybe if we arranged to meet during her lunch break.

My mind wandered so much that I almost drove right past the library. I pulled into the driveway and realized I was fifteen minutes early. I found a parking spot at the far end of the lot.

When I felt anxious as I did now, I liked to munch on snacks. Instead of asking myself why a book club triggered my anxiety, I dug in my purse and found a mini packet of trail mix. As I happily munched away, a Lexus pulled into the driveway. Sandra got out of the car and smoothed the skirt of her linen dress. How did people manage to look good in linen while I always looked as if I'd slept in it? Some things were meant to remain mysteries, I supposed.

Another car pulled in next to her and Cheryl got out. I groaned. She looked even more put together than she had at painting class. Good thing she came from a wealthy family, because she wouldn't have been able to afford her wardrobe on her husband's salary.

Before I could sink down in my seat and hide, they noticed me and waved. I brushed the crumbs off my dress and got out of the car.

"Hi, April," Cheryl called to me. "I'm so glad you came early. I can show you around and introduce you to the librarian."

I grimaced as I realized Cheryl and Sandra each held a book in their arms. "I forgot to get a copy of the book," I admitted sheepishly. I'd meant to go to my local library, but never got around to it. "Maybe I should wait and come to next month's meeting."

"No worries," Cheryl said and gestured for us to head to the front steps. "Half the time I'm too busy to read the book." In a stage whisper, she confided, "Don't tell anyone, but sometimes I just read the synopsis online."

The Somerton library didn't have the beautiful architecture of our library in Serenity Cove, but it appeared to be at least twice the size. I followed the women through the large double doors into the cavernous interior.

ONCE INSIDE THE LIBRARY, Cheryl headed for a young woman with fluffy brown hair and big glasses who stood behind a counter, grinning. I guessed she was the librarian, and it turned out I was right.

After I'd been introduced, Cheryl and Sandra headed for a meeting room near the back of the building with me following close behind. Sandra pushed the door open, and several sets of eyes looked up, including Debbie.

I counted four other women and one man sitting around a large, white conference table. Cheryl took her place at the head of the table and Debbie motioned for me to sit next to her.

A lively discussion soon took place, and I did my best to follow the conversation. Every time I glanced over at Cheryl, I had the impression she was watching me. My paranoia was really getting the better of me.

When the meeting ended, Cheryl thanked everyone for coming and announced the book for the next meeting. I hadn't heard of the author, so I wrote down the name of the book as a reminder to get a copy.

As we stood to leave, Cheryl called out to me, "April. Would you wait a moment and walk out with me?" Debbie looked surprised but left without us after Cheryl nodded curtly at her.

I waited as everyone filed out of the room. "Is there something you wanted to talk about?" I had questions for her myself, but I wasn't quite ready to ask them. She didn't answer until I'd followed her out of the room, through the library, and out the front door.

Standing on the library steps, Cheryl turned to me, narrowed her eyes, and in a deadly-quiet voice said, "Stay away from my husband."

Before I could respond, she walked off, leaving me to interpret her words. Somehow, she'd found out that the sheriff and I had been meeting in secret. Had someone seen us together and told Cheryl? No—she must have been the one who hired someone to follow her husband—or me.

But why would Cheryl have her husband or me tailed? It must have something to do with the murder. I had trouble believing my new friend had been involved, but what else was I supposed to think? I had to figure out why a socialite married to the sheriff would involve herself in something that could get her thrown in jail for a very, very long time. If she had a guilty conscience and suspected we were onto her, that might explain having us followed.

As I slowly walked down the library steps and headed for my car, an idea hit me like a ton of bricks. She thought Sheriff Fontana and I were having an affair!

~

WHEN I GOT in my car, I texted Sheriff Fontana at the number he'd used before—most likely a burner phone. I told him I thought his wife was responsible for having us followed.

Are you sure? came the response.

I didn't answer the question, nor did I share my suspicions about the reason she'd hired someone to keep an eye on us. If he didn't want to believe me, that was his problem. As I drove home, I felt my mood darken. Here I'd been hoping to find new friends and instead I had a new enemy.

I'd found enough of those since I came to town, but I'd thought I'd started to win locals over and begun to be accepted. Who was I kidding? I'd be the new person in town for at least a decade—small towns were like that.

When I arrived home, I greeted Chef and said, "I'm starving."

"Is that so?" he said. "You look well-fed to me."

The saucepan I threw went right through him and hit the tile backsplash with a loud clatter, coming to rest in the sink.

He folded his arms over his chest. "What is bothering you, ma chère?"

"I'm just feeling out of sorts." I fixed myself an egg salad sandwich and gobbled it down without tasting it. The silent house had a deserted feel without Jennifer there, and I assumed that she hadn't come home from class yet. Still, I wasn't completely alone as long as I had Chef to keep me company.

If only Emile didn't know how to push all my buttons. Sure, I'd put on a few pounds since opening the tearoom—who wouldn't? My days were spent cooking and baking, and someone had to eat the leftovers. Maybe some people could resist the temptation, but I didn't see how.

"I can't guarantee it will work for you," Chef said, pulling me from my thoughts. "But for me, nothing improves my disposition like a financier."

"A financier? I don't need financial advice." Though, if Jeff went through with his threat to hire a lawyer, that might change.

Chef shook his head in disappointment. "You have almond flour?"

I didn't know what that had to do with my finances, but I answered. "Yes, I'm sure I have some in the pantry. Why do you ask?"

He smiled indulgently and explained, "A financier is a small cake, quite unassuming in appearance, yet a delight to the taste buds."

"Is that so?" The formal way Chef expressed himself always amused me. "Okay, which cookbook is it in?"

He'd written three cookbooks when he had been

the head chef at Norma's French restaurant. I'd been through them all thoroughly but couldn't recall anything called a financier.

"The recipe is here." Chef tapped his forehead. Could he really recall a recipe he hadn't made in sixty years? Maybe he'd been in a sort of suspended animation until he appeared to me, if such a thing applied to ghosts. "Have you a financier mold?" he asked.

"I have no idea," I admitted. "What does it look like?"

"Financiers are baked in the shape of a small bar of gold, hence the name."

I stepped into the back room where every sort of pan and cooking implement could be found. They'd come with the house, which had saved me from having to buy everything. I couldn't find anything resembling his description and told him so.

"Very well," he said. "A muffin tin will do in a pinch. The first step is to make the *beurre noisette*."

"The what?"

"Brown butter."

I laughed. "It sounds so much fancier in French."

Chef instructed me in creating my first *beurre noisette*, guiding me as it began to foam and calming me down as burnt-looking bits began to appear. When it reached the perfect golden-brown color, he instructed me to pour the contents into a small bowl to cool.

After mixing the rest of the ingredients and adding in the browned butter, I poured the batter into the muffin tin and put it in the oven to bake for twenty minutes.

~

FREDDIE STOPPED by just as I took the financiers out of the oven. I breathed in the delicious aroma and my worries seemed to fade.

Freddie took a seat at the island and watched me place each cake onto a cooling rack. "If those taste half as good as they smell, you have another winner."

"They don't look all that exciting but looks can be deceiving. I want to let them cool before trying them, although I'm not sure I have that much patience. While we're waiting, would you like a cup of tea? I was about to make a pot."

"You're slipping," she said with a grin. "You used to have a pot of tea ready at any time of the day."

"True," I agreed as I scooped loose tea into the infuser. "But that was when we were open six days a week. Plus, back then, I wanted to try out every blend of tea available so I would know what to recommend to customers. Now I mostly drink the same kind every day."

"Rose petal black tea," Freddie said. "It's become my favorite too."

I poured two cups of tea and set one in front of Freddie. "Sugar?"

She shook her head. "This tea has a natural sweetness to it, don't you think?"

"I do." Lifting the cup to my lips, I took a tiny sip, careful not to burn my tongue. Setting the cup on its saucer, I asked, "Did you just stop by to see what I was baking? Or do you have news about the murder case?"

Her expression became serious. "Deputy Molina has made an arrest."

I stopped with my teacup halfway to my mouth. "He has? Who?"

"Alfred Huang. He's a business associate of Eric Vitello's. He planned to take Eric and Sandra out on his boat on Sunday. She confirmed this, as I'm sure you know."

I put my cup back on its saucer. "No, this is the first time I'm hearing this information. Cheryl told me Eric left that morning to meet with a business associate, but she didn't say anything about a boat. And Sandra went to brunch on Sunday morning."

"Sandra decided not to go with her husband at the last minute, according to her statement. The theory is that Alfred took Eric out on his boat, knocked him out, and threw him overboard."

"I see. So, case closed." Something niggled at my brain. It didn't add up. "Has he confessed?"

"No," Freddie said. "Before he lawyered up, Alfred claimed he waited at his boat for Eric, but Eric never showed. He tried to call and text but got no answer, so he went home."

"Anyone see Alfred at the marina?"

"Not a soul. It's not really a marina—just boat docks behind the homes. A lot of the owners come to Bluefish Bay for the summer to get away from the heat and the crowds. It's almost empty during the off season. The Vitellos stayed on because Sandra liked it there."

"Is there any proof that Alfred and Eric went out on the boat that Sunday? Witnesses?"

"It's Molina's investigation. You'd have to ask him."

"Right." No way would Molina share that information with me.

"Don't look so dejected," Freddie said. "You seem almost disappointed that the case is solved, and a murderer is behind bars."

"If I thought that was true, I'd be thrilled," I said.

Remembering the financiers, I put two on plates and handed one to Freddie with a fork. She pushed the plate away. "I'm meeting friends for dinner, and that will definitely spoil my appetite."

"Haven't you heard?" I said, pushing the plate back toward her. "Life's short. That's why you should eat dessert first."

She smirked but took a bite. She closed her eyes as she chewed, obviously enjoying the dessert. "Mmm."

"That sounds promising." I bit into a slightly crisp exterior that melted into a chewiness. Sweet, but not too sweet. "Chef was right again."

Freddie laughed. "You and your chef. You'd make the perfect couple if only he hadn't gone and died sixty years ago. Of course, if he didn't, he'd be over a hundred years old by now I suppose." She stood to go. "I'd better get going. I may have spoiled my appetite with that cake, but it was worth it."

"Thanks for stopping by."

Freddie waited for me as I put her plate and teacup in the sink, then gave me a hug. "Remember, leave the crime solving to the police, okay? Hunting murderers is dangerous."

"You said the murderer was in jail."

Freddie walked to the back door but turned and came back. "I think Molina has the right guy, but I can tell you don't. I'm not saying you're right, but it is possible that there's a murderer still out there. So, stay safe, okay?" Her voice and expression told me how worried she was.

I nodded solemnly. "Okay."

CHAPTER 20

The next morning, I shuffled down to the kitchen. I loved peace and quiet, especially first thing in the morning, but it made me miss Jennifer more. A glance out the window showed a dark, overcast sky. I flicked on all the lights, hoping to brighten my mood.

"Chef?" I called out softly, but he didn't answer.

I'd just started a pot of coffee when Parker knocked on the front door. My mood brightened as I hurried to let him in, happy to have the company.

"I've got coffee brewing in the kitchen." I led him through the tearoom to the back of the house. "And I always have leftovers if you're hungry."

He pulled a stool up to the island, and I served him a cup of coffee and a financier.

After one bite, he smiled. "Wow, these are amazing."

"Thanks." I had a feeling he hadn't stopped by for a snack. "What brings you here?"

"Did you hear they arrested a guy for the murder?"

"How did you find out so quickly? Is it in the news-paper?" I realized no one as young as Parker read newspapers. "Oh. You must have seen it online."

"Yeah," he said. "I've been checking every morning to see if there were any developments in the case. But they've got the wrong guy."

I thought so too but didn't want to encourage him. "Why do you say that?"

He leaned forward, his elbows on the tile. "What about the plane? And the pilot who lied about going up in the plane? And your friend knowing the pilot? What about all that?"

"Surely you don't think the sheriff's wife killed her friend's husband?" I asked. "Besides the fact that she's an upstanding member of society, she doesn't have a motive."

"But she does have a motive to help her bestie cover up a murder."

"You think that Sandra killed her husband and Cheryl is helping her get away with it? Why would she do that?"

Parker shrugged. "Sometimes friends stick together. At least some do." The sullen way he spoke made me wonder if his friends had let him down in the past.

"Everyone has their limits, and I think for most people, murder would be one step too far."

Parker sipped his coffee while he pondered my statement. "Still, you never know about people. They're unpredictable."

"True." But we had one problem. "How did Sandra manage to get Eric into the ocean while out to brunch with Cheryl and the others?" At that moment, I realized I was missing some important information. "Hang on."

I dialed Freddie and she picked up on the second ring. After a quick hello, I asked her what she'd learned about when Eric Vitello had died.

"There are many factors that go into determining time of death. It's not an exact science, and—"

"I know that, Freddie." My impatience was getting the better of me. "Just give me a window based on what you know right now."

After a pause, she said, "My best estimate at this time would be between eight A.M. the Saturday before the body was found and one P.M. the following day."

"Thanks." I hung up the phone.

Parker looked at me expectantly. "The victim wasn't murdered on Sunday, was he?"

"It's still possible," I said. "But it's also possible that he was killed on Saturday."

"And his wife doesn't have an alibi for Saturday."

"If Sandra killed her husband on Saturday, whether it was self-defense or cold-blooded murder, how did she get him into the ocean?"

Parker pulled his eyebrows together and stared at me as if the answer was obvious. "In a boat, of course."

"Right. But which boat? I haven't heard anything about the Vitellos having a boat."

"Then why do they live in Bluefish Bay?" he asked.

"What are you talking about? I thought they lived in Somerton. Bluefish Bay is an hour or two away, isn't it?"

Parker shook his head. "About twenty minutes from Somerton."

"It should be easy to see if they own a boat, I would think." I picked up my phone and did a search for their name plus "boat." No luck.

Parker said, "I already tried searching. Boat registration records are covered by privacy laws, just like car registrations. If we knew the name of the boat, we could look up the owner in the Coast Guard's database, but it doesn't work the other way around."

"I need more coffee." While I poured myself another cup, I made a plan. Find out Sandra and Eric's address and go there to see if a boat was docked behind their home. Then, armed with the name, I could look up the owner to confirm that it was their boat.

Sitting back down across from Parker, I sighed loudly. "I'll call Deputy Molina and give him the information. I'm sure he'll look into it." I doubted he would, but it was the right thing to do. If he brushed me off, I'd do my own sleuthing.

"I'm sure he won't," Parker said. "Why would he? He's already arrested someone. Someone who I believe is innocent, and I think you do too." He stood. "I thought you'd want to do the right thing."

"Let's just see what Molina says before we go jumping to conclusions. Or worse—putting ourselves in harm's way."

"Fine. Thanks for the coffee." The way he said it sounded more like, "Thanks for nothing." He got up and walked through the tearoom and out the front door.

I'd apologize to him later, but I didn't want him putting himself in danger. At his young age, chasing a murderer seemed like a fun adventure.

I knew it could be deadly.

As PROMISED, I called Deputy Molina. It turned out Parker was right, and Molina wasn't interested in what we'd learned. He claimed to know that Eric and Sandra owned a boat, but when I asked him if he'd searched it, he hung up on me.

Next, on an impulse, I called Cheryl. When she answered, I decided to see if I could bluff her into telling me the truth. I told her I knew she was covering up for Sandra.

"What are you talking about?" she asked in her most innocent voice.

"Sandra killed Eric and you helped her cover it up. Even if she killed him in self-defense, she needs to go to the authorities and turn herself in."

"You're crazy," she said, but she sounded less confident now.

"And if she won't, you should before the you-know-what hits the fan. And besides—"

Before I could finish my sentence, the phone went

dead. Two hang ups in a row had to be some kind of a record.

I searched the internet for Sandra and Eric's address, but after an hour I gave up. Darned privacy laws! When I was a kid, I could pull out a phone book and find out where anyone lived. Things sure had changed.

Next, I perused Sandra's social media account looking for clues, and finally found one. A picture of a boat, with the name, "Lovesick." After entering it in the Coast Guard database, I found lots of information but not the owner's name.

After half an hour, I gave up on finding the information online and decided a road trip was called for. Putting Bluefin Bay in my phone's navigation system, it showed a 45-minute drive from Serenity Cove via Somerton. After double checking there wasn't a short cut, I left a note for Jennifer. She might show up for work before I returned from my adventure.

I had no idea how many houses or boat docks were in Bluefish Bay, but when I took the turnoff, it appeared to be a small community—even smaller than Serenity Cove. Freddie was right about the town being quiet during the off season. Not a single car sat parked on the street or in the driveways.

Spotting the ocean, I found a place to park. When I reached the waterside, a cold wind hit me head on. No wonder few people lived here in the fall. I zipped up my sweatshirt and pulled the hood over my head.

Hugging myself in a futile attempt to stay warm, I found a walkway that led along a long row of oceanfront houses. A number of yachts and sailboats were docked behind them. I hurried by each boat, reading the names painted on the back.

The moment I read "Lovesick" on the back of what I guessed to be a 40-foot yacht, I felt a jolt of excitement. Finally! Now all I had to do was confirm that this boat belonged to the Vitellos. But then what? I'd figure out the rest of the plan later, over a nice, warm cup of tea in front of my nice, warm fireplace.

I spotted someone on the deck just before he slipped through the door into the cabin and my heart sank. I'd know that skinny kid anywhere.

"Parker!" I scolded in a whisper. I would have yelled, but I didn't want to attract attention to either of us.

After a moment of indecision, I pulled my phone out of my purse and sent him a text. *What are you doing?* Not wanting to be seen loitering where I didn't belong, I strolled further along the walk while I waited for a response. Gripping my phone tightly, I looked at the screen the moment it buzzed.

Just investigating came his answer.

Heading back to the boat, I typed my response with my thumbs: *I know. I saw you.*

A moment later, Parker's head popped out of the door and his eyes widened when he saw me. I gestured for him to get off the boat. He shook his head and retreated, closing the door behind him.

"Darn you," I mumbled before I made the impulsive decision to head out onto the dock. I had to get Parker off the boat before someone caught him. Adrenaline kicked in and I jumped onto the boat, nearly falling on my face. That would be better than falling in the ice-cold ocean.

As I reached for the cabin door, a noise behind me made me stop in my tracks. The last thing I saw as something solid met the back of my head was the teak wood flooring as I fell to the ground.

CHAPTER 21

I awoke with a splitting headache and slowly opened my eyes. As I tried to move, I became aware that I couldn't. My eyes shot wide open, as I realized I was laying on my side with my arms tied behind me. I wiggled my legs—they were tied at the ankles.

This wasn't good. Not good at all.

From my prone position, I could tell I was in a boat cabin. I assumed it was *Lovesick*. Twisting my body, I saw a pair of Converse high-tops.

"Parker?" I called out to him.

A muffled reply told me he'd been gagged. I slowly made my way to a sitting position, leaning back against the wooden base of the built-in sofa. Parker sat across from me at a dinette. He almost looked like he was getting ready to eat lunch if it weren't that his arms were tied behind his back, and he had duct tape over his mouth.

"Did they hit you, too?" I asked.

He shook his head and twisted around to show me his hands, mimicking a gun with his thumb and index finger.

"Oh." I did my best to remember what had happened before I lost consciousness. "Someone must have snuck up behind me and hit me on the back of the head. I didn't know you could really knock someone out that way. You must have heard the noise and come out to see what happened."

He nodded.

"And then she pointed a gun at you. It was a she, right? Blonde with puffy lips?"

He nodded again.

"Did she make you drag me in here?"

More nods.

"She probably made you tie me up first, then she tied you up," I said, more to myself then him. "Did she happen to mention where she was going after that?"

Parker started talking, but I couldn't understand a word.

"I don't know what you're saying." I shook my head in frustration and searing pain went through my skull from ear to ear. Parker made a sort of a whine when he saw my face contort in agony. After a few moments that felt like forever, the pain subsided.

"I'll have to remember not to do that again," I said, giving Parker a smile hoping to encourage him not to lose hope. Who was I kidding? How were we going to get out of this mess?

The frightened look on his face made my blood run

cold. When someone knocked on the cabin door, Parker jumped and stared at me with wide eyes.

We sat frozen in place as the door opened.

~

CHERYL, impeccably dressed as always, stared at me with her mouth open. "What are you doing on the floor?"

"Cheryl!" My heart full of hope, quickly turned to fear. "Wait. You're not here to finish the job, I hope."

"What are you talking about?" She stepped closer, her high heels tapping on the wood floor. "Who did this to you?"

"Who do you think?" I asked. When she returned a blank look, I explained. "Your friend, Sandra. I don't know what she has planned for us, but it isn't good. And you'd better watch out, or you'll be next."

Cheryl laughed, which unnerved me even more.

"You think this is funny?" I asked.

Parker made a moaning noise.

Cheryl noticed him for the first time. "Who are you?"

"Mmm, mmm," he said behind the duct tape.

"Oh, sorry." Cheryl reached out and yanked the duct tape off his mouth. He responded with a yelp.

"That's Parker," I said. "He's been, um," I didn't want to say helping. "He's been interested in the case."

She shot him a condescending glance, then turned back to me. "Okay, let me see if I have this right. You and your *friend* here found out where Sandra and Eric's boat was docked and what? Tied each other up? Are the police on their way even as we speak so you can tell them Sandra attacked you?"

Too bad I didn't think of calling Deputy Molina or Sheriff Fontana earlier. Come to think of it, I had called Molina, but he'd brushed me off. Would Fontana have listened? Probably not.

Cheryl continued talking. "Are they on their way so you can tell them how Sandra is a murderer and she tied you up to keep you from talking? Very creative."

"First of all," I said. "If I'd tied Parker's hands and feet and put duct tape on his mouth, how could I tie myself up? I'm not a contortionist."

"Oh." Cheryl gave me a once over. "No, you certainly aren't. You might want to consider taking some fitness classes." She took a closer look at the tightly bound ropes and shrugged. "I'm sure the two of you figured something out."

"Excuse me," Parker's trembling voice pleaded. "Can we get out of here before the crazy lady comes back?"

"Cheryl, if you'll just untie us, we'll go on home. We won't cause any more problems, I promise."

She blinked as if deciding what to do.

"Please?" Parker begged.

Cheryl shrugged. "I'm not sure if I should. You're probably going to go straight to my husband and tattle on me."

"Or you could just have a seat and wait here with us until the police show up." Bluffing was getting to be a regular thing for me. "I'd love to hear you explain this to Deputy Molina—or your husband."

Cheryl put her hands on her hips. "You just don't understand the entire situation. Sandra was living in hell. Eric tormented her. She didn't mean to kill him, but once he fell overboard, she freaked out and brought the boat home and came straight to me." She sighed. "I tried to convince her to go to the police, but she was nearly hysterical. What would you have done?"

I would have gone to the police, but I didn't say that out loud. It seemed wiser to keep my mouth shut.

Cheryl sighed again. "I guess I don't have any choice but to let you go."

She crouched down and began untying the knot, but stopped when she heard the door opened behind her. The three of us turned toward the sound.

Sandra stepped inside, her blonde hair impeccably styled and her dress as fresh as a daisy. Perhaps she'd changed her outfit after attacking me. Her narrowed eyes focused on Cheryl. "What are you doing here?"

Cheryl furrowed her brow. "I came to help you, Sandra."

Sandra tilted her head to one side. "Help?"

"She—" Cheryl gestured to me, "called me and said she knew what you'd done. I wanted to know how much she'd figured out, so I followed her. I know we were trying to keep you from having to go through the legal system, but I don't think that's an option anymore. You have the money for a good lawyer, and I can testify how Eric abused you, both physically and emotionally. I don't think you'll spend time in jail, but if you do, I'm sure it won't be more than a year or two."

"You'll go to jail too, as an accessory," Sandra said

coldly. "I'll tell everyone you helped—and not just with the coverup. Do you think your husband will stay sheriff once everything comes out? Do you think he'll stand by your side once he finds out what you've done?"

Cheryl held Sandra's gaze as she spoke barely above a whisper. "I hadn't thought of that."

"I don't know about you, but I don't want to go to jail."

Cheryl's expression and gentle voice expressed sympathy. "Of course, no one *wants* to go to jail."

"I don't think you're understanding me, Cheryl," Sandra said, the volume of her voice rising. "I am *not* going to jail, and I will do whatever it takes so that doesn't happen."

While they argued, I took advantage of their distraction to slip out of the ropes around my wrists that Cheryl had loosened. I began untying the knots around my ankles, keeping an eye on the two women.

"Whatever it takes?" Cheryl stared at Sandra, her eyes wide. "What are you saying?"

Sandra stepped closer to Cheryl. "Let's not fight. We can figure this out together."

I held my breath waiting to see what Cheryl would say. Would she really sacrifice Parker and me? As I thought about everything she had to lose, I almost felt sorry for her.

Cheryl sighed and stared out the window at the ocean beyond. "What's the plan?"

Sandra smiled with relief. "Go home and wait for me. Send your husband a text telling him we're having lunch together. As long as we stick to our stories, we'll be fine. I'll take the boat out and come back without these two."

"What if someone sees the boat?"

Sandra's eyes narrowed. "It doesn't matter. All that matters is that you and I have alibis."

"Okay," Cheryl said cheerfully. "I'll go home and wait."

As she reached for the door handle, I hoped Sandra believed her. I didn't. I expected her to call the police the moment she got far enough away.

"Will you?" Sandra asked. I'd been about to make a move when the gun appeared in Sandra's hand. If I jumped up now, Cheryl might end up with a bullet in her chest, which was where the gun was pointed. "I sense you're having a change of heart."

"Put that down," Cheryl said. "Are you really going to shoot me after everything I've done for you?"

"Throwing three people off a boat isn't much harder than two. I had planned to stay in town long enough for the insurance money to hit my account, but I've got enough to get me by for quite a while. My old partner warned me not to get greedy, rest his wicked soul." Sandra picked up a coil of rope from a shelf, never taking her eyes off Cheryl. "Turn around so I can tie you up."

Cheryl let out a piercing cry of "help!" and Sandra hit her across the jaw with the gun. She'd used enough force to fling Cheryl onto the sofa behind me.

I leapt up and threw myself at Sandra, hoping to knock her onto the ground, but I only managed to shove her against the door. She threw me aside like a rag doll.

Parker, still fully bound, jumped up, but immediately fell over onto Sandra, giving Cheryl a chance to grab Sandra's hair. Unfortunately, Sandra's perfect locks were a wig that had been covering up her short, brown hair.

"You're Jamie Jackson," I blurted out. The pieces all began to click into place in my mind. She'd created a new identity for herself, found a rich husband, and then killed him.

Parker flung himself at Sandra's legs, giving me the perfect distraction to try out my high kick. Aiming for her gun hand, I swung my leg as high as I possibly could, and the gun went flying. Sandra lunged at me but froze when she heard Cheryl's voice.

"I will shoot you," Cheryl said, holding the gun confidently pointed at Sandra. "I go to the gun range every weekend with my husband. He taught me to always aim for the heart if I'm in danger."

I grabbed the rope and tied Sandra's hands behind her extra tightly.

"Call the police," I shouted at Cheryl, not sure why she hadn't moved.

Cheryl's gun moved slightly until it pointed directly at me, and I froze. "What am I going to do about you?"

"What are you talking about?" I asked. "You don't have a lot of choices. Unless you plan to shoot all three of us,"

Parker gasped.

I took a slow breath, willing myself to stay calm.

"You're not a murderer, Cheryl. Whatever you've done up till now, I'm sure you had a good reason."

Cheryl's posture slumped and I took the gun from her, keeping it trained on Sandra as I untied Parker. Cheryl, accepting the inevitable, called for help.

I shoved Sandra onto the sofa and tied her ankles together. Then I tied her ankles to her wrists. I wasn't taking any chances.

Sirens wailed in the distance and Cheryl went out to meet the officers. Would Sheriff Fontana be among those who arrived? I couldn't wait to hear what Cheryl said when she explained everything to her husband.

CHAPTER 22

*U*nfortunately, I missed Cheryl's performance when her husband arrived along with his deputies. I imagined her running to him and throwing herself into his strong arms.

When Sheriff Fontana entered the cabin, he read Sandra, or rather Jamie, her rights and two deputies carted her off.

About that time, an ambulance arrived, and two EMTs crowded into the cabin. The sheriff stood by while they checked out Parker and me.

"I'm fine," I insisted, as one of them checked my blood pressure.

Sheriff Fontana came over to us. "Make sure you check her out thoroughly, you understand?" he told the technician. "She may have had a concussion."

"I'm fine," I repeated.

"Once they've checked you out, and no sooner, I'll want to personally question you." I got the feeling he knew more than he'd let on about his wife's role in the coverup of Eric's murder. "I'll come by the tearoom if that's okay with you."

The tearoom! I glanced at my watch and jumped up from my seat. A wave of dizziness and nausea came over me and I sat back down. "We're supposed to open in five minutes. Where's my phone?"

I heard voices outside. A low, male voice said, "You can't go in there," and a woman answered, "But I need to see April." I recognized Jennifer's young voice.

"Are we done here?" I asked the EMT.

"I highly recommend you let us take you to the emergency room, but I can't force you to go," he said, helping me slowly to my feet. He handed me an icepack. "Apply ice for fifteen to twenty minutes every hour for the next twenty-four hours. And see your personal physician as soon as possible."

I stepped out into the bright sunshine and blinked. Jennifer grinned in relief as she took my arm and led me off the boat.

"What about the tearoom?" I asked.

"I can't believe you're worried about the tearoom after nearly getting yourself killed," she said, "but on the other hand, I'm not sure why I'm surprised. I put up the closed sign. We didn't have any reservations, anyway."

When we reached her car, she opened the passenger door and helped me inside. "We'll come back and get your car later."

"I'm not an invalid," I protested as she slammed the door.

She got into the driver's seat and started the car. "If

you ever give me a scare like that, I'll... I'll..." she didn't seem able to finish her sentence, and when I looked over at her, I saw her lower lip quivering.

"I'm sorry, Jennifer," I said softly, touched by her emotion. "I'll never do anything so reckless again. Although I didn't realize it was reckless at the time, I wanted to make sure—"

"Just say you're sorry," she interrupted, "and that you won't let it happen again."

"Sorry," I said. "I won't let it happen again."

"That's better."

As she headed for home, I leaned back in my seat. "I can't wait for a nice, hot cup of tea."

FREDDIE STOOD WAITING on my front porch. She hurried down the steps as we pulled in the driveway. She opened the car door and ordered me not to move.

"The EMTs already checked me out," I said as she took my pulse.

"And recommended that you go to the emergency room, according to the sheriff."

Once she'd checked my vitals, she helped me out of the car.

"I am able to walk," I protested. "I've just had a bump on the head."

"You were knocked unconscious as I understand it," Freddie said, holding onto my arm. "You're going to listen to me and take it easy."

"Yes, ma'am."

Jennifer hurried ahead of us and held the door open. Once inside, Freddie hovered over me as I took a seat in my favorite spot on the sofa in front of the fireplace. I rubbed my arms in a feeble attempt to get the chill out of my bones.

While Jennifer made me a cup of tea, Freddie lit the fire and laid a throw blanket over my lap.

Jennifer returned with a selection of tea sandwiches. "I'm warming up some soup for you. I'm not sure what it is, but it's green."

I laughed. "Must be Caldo Verde. It literally means green broth in Portuguese. It's the kale that gives it the green flavor, but the linguiça sausage that gives it the flavor. Thanks, this looks perfect."

Molina knocked on the door and Jennifer let him in, offering him a cup of tea. For once, he accepted without asking for it to be poured over ice. She brought him his cup and returned to the kitchen.

"How are you feeling?" he asked me, taking a seat in a nearby chair.

"Just a little headachy," I answered. "And a lot stupid for walking right into a trap."

"Yeah," he said. "But if you hadn't, who knows what might have happened to your friend Parker. All's well that ends well, my mom used to say."

I stared at him, not understanding why he wasn't scolding me for investigating on my own.

"I'm sorry I didn't listen to you when you tried to tell me about Sandra," he said.

"As I recall, you hung up on me."

"Yeah, sorry about that." He bit his lower lip,

looking sheepish. "I really, really thought we had the right guy. I guess I need to learn to keep an open mind."

Another thought came to me. "Where's Sheriff Fontana? I thought he was going to come by and question me. Is he busy?" Busy with his lying wife, perhaps.

"He took himself off the case due to his wife's friendship with the alleged murderer."

"Alleged?" I heard the outrage in my voice as my pulse quickened.

Freddie came to Molina's rescue. "The police have to say 'alleged' until after the trial for legal reasons, April. It doesn't mean that anyone doubts what she did."

"And you know Cheryl Fontana helped Sandra, or Jamie, or whatever her real name is, cover up the murder, right?" I asked. "If something had happened to Parker or me, our blood would have been on her hands."

He turned to Freddie. "If you don't mind, I'd like to question Ms. May alone."

"No," she said. "It's not all right. Unless you'd prefer she call her lawyer and have him present."

"Am I in some sort of legal problem?" I asked, suddenly worried.

"No, nothing like that," Freddie said, her voice calm and reassuring. "I'm just looking out for your best interests."

"Fine, Dr. Severs," Molina said reluctantly. "You can stay, but no interruptions, please." He turned back to me. "Now, why don't you tell me everything from the beginning."

I leaned back on the sofa and thought back to when I'd first met "the girls." I'd envied the women's seemingly perfect lives at the time, especially Cheryl, with her impeccable style and her handsome, loyal husband. Poor Sheriff Fontana. I wondered how he was handling everything, considering his wife would no doubt be charged with something for her role in covering up the murder.

"I met Cheryl at art class two Wednesdays ago. She introduced me to Debbie and the person I thought was named Sandra."

Over the next hour, I told the deputy every relevant detail I could remember, including my secret meetings with Sheriff Fontana.

"That explains the rumors," he mumbled almost to himself.

"What rumors?" I asked.

He shook his head. "Nothing. Go on please."

"Tell me," I demanded, staring at him hard to let him know I meant it.

Molina looked up from his notes and huffed a sigh. "There's a rumor that you and Sheriff Fontana were having an affair."

"What?" I jumped out of my seat, but Freddie grabbed my arm and pulled me back down. "Ow." I held onto my throbbing head.

"It's just a rumor," he said. "Don't worry about it. I'm sure it won't hurt your testimony."

"Cheryl's the one who started the rumor," I said. "If she gets away with her part in this because of a rumor she started…"

"Hold on," Molina said. "No one is getting away with anything. The District Attorney in this county is tough on crime. He'll throw the book at anybody involved in murder."

"Even the sheriff's wife?" I asked.

"Even the sheriff's wife," Molina assured me.

CHAPTER 23

s it turned out, the sheriff's wife did not have the book thrown at her. Within days, we learned that Cheryl would be given immunity from prosecution in return for her testimony against Jamie Jackson.

"Well, that's not right," I grumbled to Freddie and Jennifer while I rolled out a batch of scones.

"Did you really want her to go to jail?" Freddie asked. "I can only imagine what kind of treatment a sheriff's wife would get in prison."

"I don't know," I said. "I'm just not happy with her getting off without any consequences."

The doorbell rang and Jennifer rushed off to answer it. She returned a few moments later.

"You have a visitor," she announced.

I stepped into the tearoom and found Sheriff Fontana standing next to a display of teacups. He looked very out of place.

"I wanted to stop by and see how you were," he said.

When I didn't respond right away, he added, "And to apologize."

"Apologize?" I didn't understand.

"For getting you involved in this mess. If I hadn't asked to meet you privately, maybe she wouldn't have accused us of being involved with each other."

"No big deal." Or was it. "I don't understand what you mean about getting me involved. What mess? I got myself involved in the murder investigation. And believe me, I've learned my lesson."

"Good," he said. "So, you're not upset that the rumor made you an unreliable witness?"

"What?"

"Uh oh," he said. "I thought you knew."

Everything began to make sense. "I suppose Cheryl used that to make a deal for herself. That's some woman you've got, Sheriff. I hope the two of you will continue to be very happy together."

"April, you don't understand."

"What don't I understand, Sheriff?" I asked.

Sheriff Fontana's face reddened as he did his best to control his emotions. "I married her for better or worse. That promise meant something to me when I made it. I may regret it for as long as I live, but I will stand by my wife."

We stared at each other, and my heart began to break for him. "I'm sorry," I whispered.

"Me too." He turned and walked out the door.

∾

DESPITE HAVING Cheryl ready to testify at Jamie Jackson's trial, the District Attorney called me in for a deposition to learn what I knew. Irma offered to drive me to Somerton, and I happily took her up on her offer.

While she waited for me, I was hit with a barrage of questions. After an hour of having every statement I made torn apart, I felt like I was the one standing trial.

By the time Irma drove me back home, she could tell it hadn't been an easy session.

"Do you want to talk about it?" she asked.

"No," I answered, and we drove the rest of the way in silence.

Irma dropped me off on her way to work. She invited me to stop by the Mermaid Cafe for dinner.

"Thanks, but I think I'll stay in tonight." I felt drained and depleted from the day's events. "Maybe take a long bath."

I unlocked my front door and entered, calling out, "Jennifer?" Silence greeted me. I stepped back onto the front porch and took a seat on the porch swing. Rocking back and forth, I gazed out at the ocean, watching the waves roll in.

"April May, you have no reason to feel sorry for yourself," I told myself, but I hadn't felt so lonely in a long time. Jennifer had moved out, Irma was busy with her restaurant, and Freddie had an active social life that filled up her non-working hours.

Even my cat, if I could call Whisk mine, preferred his own company.

I thought a new hobby would help fill the void, but

it had only brought problems. My mother would have told me to find a good man, but that was easier said than done. It seemed like I had a knack for finding Mr. Wrong.

A tear trickled down my cheek, and I brushed it away. I had everything I thought I wanted, a lovely home, a wonderful business, friends, and yet...

Another tear. I sniffled and scolded myself for crying. Maybe I needed to get away for a few days. A trip to San Francisco perhaps. Or a spa retreat. The thought did little to cheer me.

The door opened behind me, and I nearly jumped out of my skin before I realized it was Jennifer.

"I thought I heard you come home," she said. "It's lovely out here. A little chilly. I'll be right back."

She returned moments later with two throw blankets and handed me one.

"I didn't realize you were here," I said. "I figured you'd be with your grandmother."

"Yeah, about that," she said, her mouth curling into a smile. "Did you know that no matter how much you love someone, they can really get on your nerves? She practically follows me around all day. 'Have you eaten?' 'Where are you going?' 'Don't you think you should wear a sweater?'"

I chuckled. "I know exactly what you mean."

"Um..." Jennifer hesitated. "Would it be okay with you if I didn't move out after all?"

"That would be more than okay." A little spark of happiness danced in my chest.

Freddie's car pulled into the driveway. The

passenger door flung open, and Irma called out, "Somebody wanna help me with all this?"

Jennifer told me to stay put as she hurried over to take a shopping bag from Irma. Freddie carried what looked like bottles of champagne.

"Irma said you had a rough day, so we decided we'd bring dinner to you," Freddie said. "Lobster bisque for starters and prime rib with all the fixings."

I grinned. They could have brought chicken nuggets and I'd have been happy just to have them there.

"Shall we go inside?" I asked.

My three friends set up the table and served the food, leaving me with nothing to do but enjoy the scrumptious feast.

I picked up my champagne flute. "Here's to friends. I don't need anyone else in my life but you three."

A hiss came from the staircase, and we all turned to see Whisk looking perturbed, his whiskers twitching.

I pushed back my chair. "Excuse me. I meant to say, I don't need anyone but you *four*."

Whisk scampered over and jumped into my lap. He kneaded my thighs before curling up in a ball.

"He's probably after your lobster," Irma said, but I knew better.

Whisk felt the warmth that came from friends who cared about each other and always came to each other's aid without being asked. Friends who believed in me more than my own family ever did. I blinked back tears as I grinned at Irma, Jennifer, and Freddie, and felt Whisk purring on my lap.

Something caught my eye, and I turned to see Chef

standing in the kitchen doorway. His smile expressed contentment and longing. Even in his ghostly form, I'd come to regard him as family. I blew him a kiss. A glow surrounded his ghostly body and I gasped.

"What is it?" Jennifer asked.

"I'm just happy," I said. "Happy to have all of you here with me. You're like family to me."

Irma grunted. "We are family. You're stuck with us, so you'd better get used to it."

Families came in all shapes and sizes. I wouldn't trade my new family for all the tea in China.

EPILOGUE

*I*rma and I continued our daily walks on the beach, dressing more warmly as Halloween approached. I dropped out of dance class, since high kicks brought back unsettling memories of having a gun pointed at me.

One afternoon a few weeks later, Jennifer returned with the mailbox with something for me.

"You have a letter," she said, handing me a pink envelope.

I grinned as I glanced at the curly script spelling out my name. "I always love getting letters. But who sends them anymore?"

"My grandmother," Jennifer said. "She sends letters to her friends back in Ohio. I ask her why she doesn't just call them, but she says it's just not the same."

"She might have a point." Unfolding the flowery pages, I read the letter.

. . .

DEAR APRIL,

I'm sorry I haven't written sooner, but I didn't know what to say. You were so kind to me, and I was mean. I'm not a mean person, so I hope you'll forgive me.

Jeff and I had a long talk on the long drive home. I was so upset I almost moved out. Then I had some news, so I decided to do my best to make my marriage work.

You're going to be an aunt!

Jeff agreed that we won't talk about the inheritance again. I never wanted a big diamond anyway! I'm going back to my job as a preschool teacher and somehow, we'll make ends meet.

I hope you will invite us to come visit again. I'm hoping we can stay in your beautiful guest room.

Your sister,

Lulu May

FROM THE AUTHOR

Thank you for reading Tea is for Traitor.

If you'd like to learn what happens next, preorder Tea is for Tears, the next Haunted Tearoom Cozy Mystery on Amazon

Sign up for mostly weekly updates, with pictures, giveaways, and other fun stuff at https://karensuewalker.com.

You can see all my books at https://karensuewalker.com/books.

And read on for recipes!

RECIPES

Caldo Verde (Portuguese Kale Soup)
6 servings

Ingredients:

- 2 Tablespoons unsalted butter
- 6 Tablespoons olive oil
- 1 medium onion diced
- 3 garlic cloves minced
- Salt and pepper
- 12 oz. cooked linguiça sausage hot or mild, cut into ¼ to ½ inch slices (or another smoked sausage such as chorizo or andouille).
- 1 large russet potato, cut into small chunks (around one inch)
- 2 medium Yukon Gold potatoes (or other yellow skin variety) cut into small chunks (one inch or so)

- 6 cups chicken stock
- 1 bunch curly kale (about ¾ lb.), stems removed and chopped or torn into small pieces

Directions:

1. Melt butter in large saucepan or Dutch oven with olive oil over medium heat, then add onion, garlic, salt, and pepper. Stir frequently for about 5 minutes until softened (not browned).
2. Brown sausages in pan, then remove and set aside until the last step.
3. Add potatoes and stock to pan. Bring to a simmer, stirring occasionally.
4. Add kale and cook 25 to 30 minutes until the russet potatoes are falling apart and the Yukon gold potatoes are tender.
5. Stir in sausage, season with salt and pepper to taste, and serve.

April's note: The key to how spicy this soup is will depend on the sausage you pick, so choose carefully!

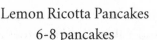

Lemon Ricotta Pancakes
6-8 pancakes

- 2 eggs, separated

- 1 ¼ cups all-purpose flour
- 1 teaspoon baking soda
- 1 teaspoon baking powder
- ½ teaspoon salt
- 2 Tablespoons white sugar
- 1 cup ricotta (regular or reduced fat)
- ¾ cup whole or reduced fat milk (nonfat not recommended)
- ½ teaspoon lemon juice and zest of one lemon (vanilla can be substituted for the lemon)
- 1 Tablespoon butter, coconut oil, or other light oil for frying
- Additional butter for serving if desired
- Maple syrup or other topping—fruit, jam, or honey are all delicious!

Directions:

1. Whisk egg whites briskly in a small bowl or measuring cup until slightly foamy (they don't need to be beaten into peaks).
2. In a large bowl, whisk together dry ingredients—flour, baking soda, baking powder, salt, and sugar.
3. In another bowl, whisk ricotta, milk, lemon and zest (or vanilla), and egg yolks until fairly smooth.
4. Add the ricotta mixture to the flour mixture and mix gently—there should still be some lumps.

5. Gently mix in the egg whites into the mixture and allow the batter to set while warming your skillet or griddle.

6. Heat skillet or griddle greased with butter over medium heat or set electric griddle at 375 F. You'll know it's ready when a drop of water skips on the surface.

7. Use ¼ or 1/3 cup measuring scoop to place dollops of batter in the hot skillet. Cook about 90 seconds to 2 minutes until bubbles begin forming on the surface. (They won't pop as much as regular pancakes do because of the thickness of the ricotta.) Flip and continue to cook until heated throughout. Repeat with remaining batter.

8. Serve warm with butter, syrup, and/or toppings.

∼

Flourless Fudge Cookies (gluten free)
Makes about 18

Ingredients:

- 3 large egg whites
- 2 teaspoons vanilla extract
- 2 ¼ cups confectioners' sugar (aka powdered or icing sugar)
- 1 cup cocoa powder
- ¼ teaspoon salt

- 1 cup chocolate chips or chopped nuts

Directions:

1. Preheat oven to 350 F (180 C)
2. Line 2 cookie sheets with lightly greased (oil or butter) parchment paper.
3. Whisk together egg whites and vanilla.
4. Mix confectioners' sugar, cocoa, and salt
5. Add egg white mixture to dry ingredients and mix thoroughly, scraping bowl. Batter will be very sticky.
6. Fold in chips or nuts.
7. Drop rounded tablespoons onto prepared cookie sheets and let rest for about 30 minutes.
8. Bake for 9-10 minutes and allow to cool on cookie sheet.

Chickpea Curry Stew (vegan)
4 servings

Ingredients:

- 1-2 cups cooked rice—your favorite unflavored white or brown rice—basmati or jasmine is great for this dish
- 1 Tablespoon coconut oil
- 1 large red onion, thinly sliced

- Pinch salt
- 3 cloves garlic, minced (about 1 Tablespoon)
- 1 Tablespoon minced or grated fresh ginger (can substitute ½ teaspoon ground ginger)
- 1 Tablespoon garam masala (this is the main spice giving this dish its wonderful flavor, so don't skip or substitute!)
- ¼ teaspoon ground turmeric
- ¼ tsp ground black pepper (less if fresh ground)
- ¼ teaspoon salt
- 14-ounce can diced tomatoes, drained (approximately 1 ½ cups)
- 14-ounce can full-fat coconut milk (approximately 1 ½ cups) Must be canned—don't use coconut milk that comes in a carton--it's much thinner and meant for drinking, not cooking
- 16-ounce can cooked chickpeas, drained and rinsed (about 1 ¾ cups)
- 2 Tablespoons freshly-squeezed lime (or lemon) juice from 1-2 limes

Directions:

1. Measure and prep all ingredients before starting—there won't be spare time to do it while cooking!
2. Heat coconut oil over medium-high heat in large pan (Dutch oven, large saucepan, or skillet with high sides).

3. Add red onion and pinch of salt and cook, stirring frequently until onion begins to brown.

4. Reduce heat to medium and add garlic and ginger, stirring for one minute.

5. Add garam masala, turmeric, black pepper, cayenne pepper, and salt. Cook for 30 seconds to toast the spices.

6. Add drained tomatoes, stir and cook for a few minutes until the tomatoes begin to break down and begin to look somewhat dry.

7. Stir in coconut milk and chickpeas. Bring to a boil, then lower heat and simmer for 10 minutes. Stir in fresh lime juice and add additional salt to taste if desired.

8. Serve hot over rice and enjoy!

Financiers (Almond Cakes)
12 cakes

Ingredients

- 150 grams (10 ½ Tablespoons) unsalted butter
- 50 grams (1/3 cup) all-purpose flour
- 125 grams (1 ¼ cup) almond meal or almond flour
- 80 grams confectioners' (icing/powdered) sugar

- Pinch salt
- 5 egg whites
- 1 teaspoon vanilla extract
- Slivered almonds (optional, to taste)

Directions:

1. Preheat oven to 325F/160C and grease Financier or muffin pan.
2. Brown the butter by first melting it in a small saucepan over low to medium-low heat. Cook until butter foams, then stir constantly for about 4-6 minutes until the melted butter turns golden and has a nutty aroma. You should see brown specks at the bottom of the pan. Set aside to cool.
3. In large bowl, mix flour, almond meal or almond flour, confectioners' sugar, and salt.
4. In medium bowl, lightly whisk the egg whites until they begin to froth, then mix in vanilla.
5. Add eggs/vanilla and browned butter to dry ingredients and mix gently until smooth.
6. Fill financier pan or muffin tin about ½ or ¾ full and smooth top.
7. Sprinkle slivered almonds on top and bake for about 20 minutes until lightly golden.
8. Let cool in pan for ten minutes then transfer to cooling rack.

April's note: I highly recommend using a scale for the measurements—it's much more reliable. A digital scale isn't very expensive and takes up little space in your kitchen.

~

I hope you enjoyed Tea is for Traitor and the recipes! I had a lot of fun writing the story and testing the recipes. Tea is for Tears is the next book in the series, and you can preorder it now on Amazon.

Did you know that if you sign up for weekly emails, you'll get free stories, bonus content, news about sales, and lots of pictures of my rescue dog Kit? By the way, Kit is featured in a new series coming in Summer 2022, and you can download the prequel *The Black Daiquiri* on my website at https:// karensuewalker.com/kcwalker.

Made in United States
North Haven, CT
04 August 2023

39880062R00125